CUTTHROAT COMPETITION

Some people think Alfred Hitchcock has it easy as the world's greatest connoisseur of diabolical mystery and suspense. But Alfie doesn't feel that way.

Every time he thinks he's discovered the ultimate in monstrously cunning evil, along comes a fresh contender—with a delicious new poison, or a novel method of strangulation, or a modern miracle of murderous technology.

Still, picking the best ones isn't the hardest part. The really painful task is getting rid of all the sore losers. Of course, if anyone knows how to do it, Alfie's the one. . . .

But enough shop talk. It's time to take a shivering look at the winners in—

ALFRED HITCHCOCK'S

Murders on the Half-Skull

MURDERS ON THE HALF-SKULL

ALFRED HITCHCOCK

EDITOR

A DELL BOOK

ACKNOWLEDGEMENTS

ONE NOVEMBER NIGHT BY *Jack Webb*—Copyright © 1969 by H. S. D. Publications, Inc. Reprinted by permission of the author and the author's agents, Scott Meredith Literary Agency, Inc.

THE ALREADY DEAD BY *C. B. Gilford*—Copyright © 1967 by H. S. D. Publications, Inc. Reprinted by permission of the author and the author's agents, Scott Meredith Literary Agency, Inc.

#8 BY *Jack Ritchie*—Copyright © 1958 by H. S. D. Publications, Inc. Reprinted by permission of the author, Larry Sternig Agency, and Scott Meredith Literary Agency, Inc.

THE DAY OF THE EXECUTION BY *Henry Slesar*—Copyright © 1957 by H. S. D. Publications, Inc. Reprinted by permission of the author and the author's agent, Theron Raines.

WHO HAS BEEN SITTING IN MY CHAIR? BY *Helen Nielsen*—Copyright © 1960 by H. S. D. Publications, Inc. Reprinted by permission of the author and the author's agents, Scott Meredith Literary Agency, Inc.

CONTENTS

INTRODUCTION

Sitting at breakfast next to Carlton Hugo, the eminent criminologist—obviously I've chosen a false name to avoid lawsuits—I asked him if he could supply me with a more precise definition for what is loosely termed the "criminal type."

"Time does not permit it," he said. "There are altogether too many aspects and factors to consider."

I was dismayed, but not crushed. "Allow me to restate my question," I said. "Is there a distinct physical criminal type?"

He nodded. "There is. I take a sharp exception to those critics who say that Lombroso delayed for fifty years the work of criminologists, inasmuch as he had never made a study of criminals and noncriminals."

"How fascinating," I said.

"All right then, Lombroso said criminals are by birth a distinct type, which can be recognized by stigmata, or anomalies, such as a flattened nose, long lower jaw, meager beard, asymmetrical cranium and low sensitivity to pain. Over the years, however, the Lombroso school of thought has tended to disappear, but I've always known it for a fact that his words were true. You can actually find his types by merely walking the streets and looking at people."

I was astounded by this statement from so authoritative a source. "You mean," I said, "that if I find people with flattened noses and long lower jaws that I will have actually found criminal types?"

He thought for a long time before replying. "Yes and no. There are exceptions. It isn't a hard and fast rule. Of course, there is one sure method of finding them without any chance of error." And then he fell silent.

"I will be forever in your debt if you will tell me," I said.

"All right then, but I must have your word that you will not divulge this secret."

I hastened to assure him that I could be trusted and without further ado he said, "You can find criminal types at wrestling matches. All you have to do is look at the spectators. Watch their snarling faces and you'll be able to detect criminal types immediately."

"It seems so simple," I replied. "But surely not all of those snarling people are criminal types."

"Regard those who are for the villains, those who are for evil over good. You can recognize them at once. Look for long jaws and flattened noses. They're a dead giveaway."

For weeks his words plagued me. Was it possible that his theories were correct? Finally, I could stand it no longer. I called and asked if I could accompany him the next time he went to the wrestling matches and he said that he'd be delighted.

A week later we went to a local arena and attended what was billed as a professional wrestling exhibition. The wrestlers, or actors, whichever you prefer, were faultlessly cast and clearly defined.

Good was Mister Everyman, a puzzled, head-scratching type, battling his adversary, Evil. Evil was a neck-stomping, eye-gouging, villainous type who managed to get his dirty work in while the referee remained oblivious to what was happening.

The crowd viewed it angrily, shouting uncouth statements at the villain which I noted did not in any way disturb his stoic expression or cool aplomb.

I studied the shouting, snarling faces around me and

determined that there were more of them rooting for Good than for Evil. Good triumphed in the first two encounters, then Evil won the next two contests. The last match of the evening was between the Ape, a great, hairy, brooding man in black tights representing Evil, and a baby-faced young man named Purefox in a green and gold sequined cape, obviously representing Good.

From the beginning the Ape was merciless, kicking Purefox repeatedly in the kidneys, head and thorax, eye-gouging at will, and stomping him while shouting, "Die! Die, Purefox!" Alternately leering and mouthing silent words of deprecation at his detractors in the crowd, the Ape aroused them to a huge emotional state of anger, which in turn evoked hissing, booing and rather sharp rejoinders. Altogether, it was a most disgusting exhibition on the part of the Ape, I thought.

Purefox was one of those ill-starred fellows who seemed always to be blundering into difficulty. Whatever Purefox tried met with failure. When he'd bounce off the ropes in an effort to throw a body block at the Ape, the Ape would adroitly dodge and Purefox would hurtle out of the other side of the ring. Invariably he landed atop the spectators, who pummeled him in disgust before he could return to the ring.

I was resolved to be completely objective. Nevertheless, I soon found myself cheering for Purefox the underdog. No man deserved to take such punishment.

I rose from my seat in the second row and shouted, "Respond, Purefox! Respond! Have a go at him!," meanwhile ignoring some spectators who were shouting, "Down in front!"

Purefox heard me. He stood in midring, scratching his head and staring intently at me. And then, encouraged by my words, he lifted the Ape over his head, whirled him about once or twice and sent him flying from the ring.

In one glance I saw it all: the Ape airborne, snarling wide-eyed, nostrils flared, expression desperate. I was able to determine the direction of his flight. In one horror-filled moment I knew he was on a collision course with Carlton Hugo. At the last moment Hugo attempted to avoid him. It was too late! He fell backward under the great, sweaty weight of the Ape—three hundred and sixty-five pounds, as I judged it—and Hugo's chair crumpled and splintered. Laughter erupted all around us.

Carlton Hugo howled angrily. His nose as well as his dignity had been flattened. The grimly visaged Ape returned to the ring. Then, to my astonishment, I heard Carlton Hugo cheering for the Ape. Cheering for Evil. "Go on, Ape!" he shouted over and over again.

I am distressed to report that the Ape triumphed over Purefox, due no doubt to Carlton Hugo's strong words of encouragement.

Driving home with the criminologist, I spent long minutes studying him. While his lower jaw wasn't especially long, his head was definitely asymmetrical and his nose had been flattened. It was enough for me. Here was irrefutable proof. I had found a distinct physical criminal type, Carlton Hugo, the criminologist. The point I have made is that you can occasionally find criminal types when you least expect to.

And now that I have revealed this sparkling bit of knowledge, I would be honored if you would read the stories that follow, whose characters will offer even more hidden insight into the world of criminal behavior and types.

—ALFRED HITCHCOCK

ONE NOVEMBER NIGHT

by Jack Webb

Lyle Beckwith was a methodical man who believed that one could organize the future as well as the present. One organized the future simply by foreseeing and being prepared for all eventualities. Even the eventuality of being assaulted and robbed on the street.

Such violence was a possibility in Lyle Beckwith's life, because on one night every week he had to be out on the streets. On that night, usually Monday, he didn't go home to dinner. Instead, he drove over to the other side of town where he kept the books for Garman's Market. Mr. Garman paid Lyle fifteen dollars a week for this service—pretty good pay, Lyle figured, for about three hours' work. And it was a rather important fifteen dollars, because it bought music lessons for his daughters, Sandra and Sheila, plus a few other small extras—and all without disturbing the "basic Beckwith budget."

Against that tidy little weekly sum Lyle had weighed the dangers. Garman's Market was one block off Majestic, which was a well-lighted, well-traveled thoroughfare. Lyle had to think of the safety of his automobile, too, so he thought it best to park on Majestic, preferably right under a street light. He would usually arrive at the market about seven, and he would leave between ten and ten-thirty. Theoretically, then, his only real risk was the one-block walk from the market to Majestic Avenue about ten o'clock at night. Surely the risk was small.

But he had a plan of action ready just the same. This plan involved his briefcase, a battered old black job with a reluctant zipper. Lyle carried the thing with him to work every day, but it was really misleading. Lyle was not important enough at his office to be required to take papers home in the evening and pore over them. The briefcase was only a camouflage for his lunch—and on Mondays his dinner, too. The savings from this little practice had bought braces for Sandra's teeth. But since he was a white-collar man, Lyle thought carrying a lunch pail was somewhat degrading. Besides, he was a small man, and thin in the bargain, so the briefcase also lent a certain air of distinction.

Moreover, the briefcase was the key to his plan of defense. He had a perfect horror of physical violence. And should he be accosted by holdup men, he certainly didn't want to be on the receiving end of any of the kind of rough stuff he read about in the papers—not to mention what it would cost him if the would-be bandits broke his glasses or anything like that.

All that could be avoided, Lyle figured, by sacrificing the briefcase. When the bandit approached—and Lyle was sure he would recognize the type—he would simply throw his briefcase at him, yell, "Here, you can have it!" and run. The implication of "Here, you can have it!" would be obvious. The briefcase contained valuables of some kind, but the owner would rather surrender those valuables than try to resist. What bandit in his right mind would pursue the man and not stop for the briefcase? Lyle had read somewhere that a man who had been held up had scattered some money on the ground which his assailants stopped to pick up, enabling the man himself to escape. Lyle reckoned that the bait of the briefcase was just as good. And with that reluctant zipper, it would take somebody a long time to get a peek inside the thing, and that would give Lyle plenty of time for retreat. Besides, the briefcase was cheaper than new glasses, and maybe too he could get Mr. Garman to buy him a new one.

A foolproof plan, with perhaps even a positive advantage. All one had to do, Lyle figured, was to be prepared for all eventualities.

On this brisk, chilly night in November, Lyle Beckwith left Mr. Garman's premises confidently. He was dressed in a gray topcoat and a gray felt hat, not recently blocked, and he carried his briefcase. With the purposeful stride of a man who has somewhere to go, he walked toward Majestic Avenue.

As always on these Monday nights, he was alert and suspicious. He kept a sharp lookout for other pedestrians, determined to give them all a wide berth, not to let anybody get so close to him that he couldn't pull his briefcase routine.

The journey promised to be uneventful. He seemed to be alone on the sidewalks. Nevertheless, when he reached the corner at Majestic, he paused for a moment and glanced around in all directions, up and down the street, right and left. His car was parked half a block down Majestic, and the space between it and him appeared to be empty. He turned with military precision and marched in that direction.

But he hadn't taken more than a dozen steps when the whole picture changed. Twenty feet ahead of him, out of the shadows of the line of parked cars, two men stepped. Lyle halted instantly, and so did the men.

With his glasses, Lyle's eyesight was keen enough. And what he saw about the two men wakened his primitive instincts of fear and self-preservation. The men were not of a size—one was much taller and leaner than the other—but they were dressed similarly. Each wore a hat with the brim turned down. Each wore a topcoat, and each had both his hands thrust into the pockets of his coat. They both stood as still as statues, waiting for Lyle to come up the sidewalk.

It wasn't quite as Lyle had foreseen it. The men weren't supposed to be dressed like a couple of private

eyes or foreign correspondents, and they were supposed
to approach him more furtively and ask for a match or
something like that. Yet Lyle felt no ebb of confidence.
His plan of battle would adjust easily to this change of
strategy by the enemy.

For a long moment, the antagonists faced one another. Lyle's flabby, civilized muscles tensed for what
he knew must surely come. If he would not go to the
men, they certainly would come to him. So he was
ready when they took their first tentative steps.

"Here, you can have it!" he shouted, and he threw
the briefcase at them.

He did not wait to see where the poor bag landed
or the men's reaction to the maneuver. While the briefcase was still in midair, he whirled and ran down Majestic Avenue in the opposite direction.

For a second or two, his own footsteps made the only
sounds in the quiet night. He had definitely taken the
marauders completely by surprise. In his mind's eye he
imagined the pair, first staring down at their booty so
easily claimed, then seeing their victim receding down
the street, finally saying, "The heck with him," and
greedily stooping to examine their treasure. And that
zipper—that good ol' zipper, his ace-in-the-hole—delaying them and delaying them till their quarry was
safely out of reach.

Just how much of this routine the two men followed
Lyle never exactly knew. But he had scarcely regained
the corner when it first began to appear that his plan
had somehow gone awry. For the footsteps of those men
were pounding on the sidewalk behind him.

The realization couldn't hasten him any because he
was already moving faster than he ever had in the past
twenty years. But the fact that he was being pursued
didn't stop him either. He flew across the street and
hurtled down Majestic's next block. Still he didn't realize how far things had gone amiss until the next several
events happened in quick succession.

"Stop, or we'll shoot!"

He didn't stop.

Three shots rang out, and things like bees buzzed past his ears.

Lyle knew then that his plan, however it might have comforted him for the past six months, had somehow fizzled. And from that point on he proceeded without plan, using every instinct and bit of primitive cunning which lies dormant within the mind and body of every twentieth-century bookkeeper.

The echo of the third shot hadn't died when Lyle forsook the sidewalk and dove for shelter in the darkness between two parked cars. He crouched there for a second, panting, all his senses finely tuned.

Majestic Avenue was profoundly silent. He knew the men hadn't abandoned the chase. He seemed to have confused them at least. Probably they didn't know his exact whereabouts. He raised himself a bit so that he could peer through the car windows to check on theirs.

Then he saw them. They were standing on the sidewalk about five or six cars down from the car that sheltered him. One had the briefcase. Both had guns, he was sure. He couldn't exactly see the guns, but he could tell from the way they held their right hands, waist high and thrust forward.

How long would they pursue him? he asked himself. How anxious were they to get hold of him? And why? He was no expert on the strange workings of the criminal mind, so he couldn't imagine their motivations. They had the briefcase—one of the men was carrying it. What more did they want? Him, of course. But were they angry at the way he had outsmarted them? Or were they perhaps—and this thought really chilled him —the sadistic kind of criminal who sought the pleasure of inflicting injury rather than financial gain?

He had little time to speculate on these horrible possibilities. One of the men—the one without the briefcase—was sidling over to the curb, inching cautiously between two cars, and approaching the street side of the line of parked vehicles. The pincers technique. They were trying to surround him.

Lyle reacted instantly, without premeditation. Leav-

ing cover and dashing out to the open of either the
street or the sidewalk would have only made him a
target. So he did the only thing there was to do. He
flattened himself on the ground, then propelled himself
forward, face down, using his elbows and knees for
traction in a way that would have delighted a Marine
training sergeant, and wriggled completely under one
of the automobiles.

He well knew how helpless he would be if discovered in that position, but he tried not to think of it. He
lay there and held his breath, his mind blank but the
springs in his body still coiled to move in any direction.

He had concealed himself just in time. He heard soft
footfalls from two directions. They told him clearly
what was happening. One man was coming down the
sidewalk, the other down the street. They were moving
at the same cautious speed, like G.I.'s in movies he had
seen, working as a team into a boobytrapped town.
Then they stopped, still synchronized, one on either side
of the car he was under. For a drawn-out interval there
was utter silence.

"Where'd he go, Mike?" came a whisper finally.

"Thought it was somewhere about here," the voice
belonging to Mike whispered back.

"Do you see him?"

"No."

"Don't think he got into one of these cars, do you?"

"We'd have heard the door."

Lyle shivered as he waited for the inevitable. All
they had to do was have a different preposition occur
to them, change "into one of these cars" to *"under* one
of these cars." It was a switch in the thought direction
of one of the men that saved him.

"Charley, take a look into that briefcase while you've
got a chance."

"Can't get the bum zipper open."

Bless that bum zipper! If Charley looked into that
briefcase and found only a lunch box and a thermos
bottle, they'd really be mad.

"Well, hold onto it anyway."

"I'm not letting go of it."

"He could have sneaked farther down the line on the street side, before I came around here. I think he's farther down. Let's keep going."

The voices stopped, and the footsteps continued on. Lyle waited till there was silence again. He had decided one thing. Pretty soon they'd think of looking *under* cars, and he didn't want to be where he was when they did. Using the same wormlike means of locomotion, he inched out from beneath the car on the street side. His pursuers, he saw, were eight or nine cars down the street. So it was back in the other direction for him. He straightened up and began his retreat with the best combination of silence and speed that he could manage.

When he reached the corner again, he had to make a decision, whether to continue down Majestic Avenue toward his car or to turn right toward Garman's Market, hoping that Mr. Garman would still be there and let him in. Without any particular reason, trusting to luck, he chose the latter course.

He increased his pace to a run now. One block to go . . . you'd think somebody would have heard those shots and would have called the police . . . but there were mostly small stores in this immediate area . . . all shut up for the night now . . . would Mr. Garman still be at the market?

What happened next, however, made that last question of no concern. Lyle was halfway down the block, full of momentum, when he saw the two men appear under the street light at the far corner. He lurched to a stop by swerving into the wall of a building. He stayed there a moment, staring at the men.

They weren't Charley and Mike, who were, as far as he knew, still walking down the line of parked cars on Majestic Avenue. And yet these two looked just like Charley and Mike, with the topcoats and the turned down hats. And the way they held their fists forward meant they had guns.

Either coincidentally another pair of toughs, Lyle thought wildly, or part of the same gang. But it scarcely made any difference. He knew somehow that they were after him, or if luckily they hadn't seen him yet, at least they would soon be after him. And he didn't have a briefcase to distract this pair.

He hesitated only long enough to see that they were coming toward him at a fast trot. Then he turned and ran. His gray topcoat must have been light enough for the men to see him. They yelled something. He couldn't hear what they had yelled, above the sound of his own running, and he didn't stop to find out. There were two shots. More bees in the air, buzzing above his head.

He was back on Majestic Avenue now. To his left, down the block, he thought he saw movement. Presumably Charley and Mike. Lyle turned right.

As he did so, he was aware of the headlights of a car coming down the side street, not from the direction of Garman's Market and his second pair of pursuers, but from the other way. It was coming fast and it was going to turn into Majestic.

Lyle did some quick thinking. This was the only car he had seen on Majestic since the chase began, and it might be the last he would see. As it lunged into its fast turn, he darted out toward it, waving his arms like a drowning man.

The driver must have seen him, because the brakes screeched. Even so, the car was going so fast that it hurtled thirty or forty feet beyond Lyle before it quivered to a full stop. He ran in pursuit of it.

Only to halt once again in full flight. Because he saw doors on each side of the car open and a third pair of men in topcoats and turned down hats emerge from them. Their fists were also clenched around what undoubtedly were guns.

Despair hit Lyle full in the face now. This thing had all the horror of a nightmare. A pair of gunmen in every direction he turned. Yet he knew it was real. Terribly real. And he was only a little undersized, underweight bookkeeper who couldn't do a dozen push-ups. Why didn't he give up?

But he didn't. As far as he knew, he had no ancestors at Thermopylae or the Little Big Horn. It was just the plain cussedness in him that makes all human beings of whatever size or kind want to stay alive.

He turned to his left now, steering a middle course between the second and third pairs of gunmen, the ones from the car and the ones from the direction of Garman's Market. To his far, far left, Charley and Mike might be closing in, too.

He ran across to the other side of Majestic, half-surrounded but not yet trapped. Ahead of him in the gutter lay a brick. He didn't throw the brick, but used it as a hammer against a store's plate-glass front. Three smashes against the glass in a vertical line, then some shoving with his topcoat-protected shoulder, and he was through the glass without a scratch.

Inside the store, Lyle acted with the instinctive cunning of a weasel in a chicken house with the farmer coming through the door. He knew that, if his pursuers had shot at him, they wouldn't hesitate following him into the store. And he knew also that he couldn't indefinitely evade a gang of six armed men.

He didn't know what kind of store it was. He only knew that he toppled over several racks of some kind of merchandise as he ploughed through the place. A small square patch of darkness not as dark as the rest of the black interior beckoned him toward the rear door.

When he got there, to his surprise, he saw that the door was ajar. He pushed it wide open, but instead of exiting through it, he flung his body to the floor, rolled a few times, and then lay still.

He'd been just in time. From where he lay, he saw two men arrive at the front of the store, hesitate, then pick their way gingerly through the man-sized hole in the glass.

"Look," a voice said, "the back door's open. He went out that way."

They blundered through the store toward Lyle, tripping over the things that he had knocked down, curs-

ing as they came. They passed within two steps of his
prone body. They didn't even hesitate at the door, to
question whether the person they were after had really
gone out the door. They simply ran out into the back
alley, and in a moment had completely disappeared.

All was quiet. Lyle lay where he was and rested.
Somewhere outside the six would converge and then
begin to wonder where their man had slipped by them,
and then maybe they would backtrack.

So he couldn't rest where he was too long. After a
minute or so, he got up and began picking his way toward the front of the store. He still had the brick somehow, dangling heavily from his fingers and dragging his
whole arm down with it. And he continued to hold onto
it for he might need it.

He paused at the broken glass before trying to go out
through it. Majestic Avenue seemed empty, of cars, of
gunmen, of anything that lived and moved. Empty and
safe. Or was the emptiness deceptive? He had been surprised several times too often this evening. He'd wait
a moment longer and see.

It was while he was waiting there, staring suspi-
ciously out, that his sharpened instincts told him that
some kind of danger lurked inside the store. He froze,
and his fingers clenched tightly around the brick. He
was no longer tired, but tense and prepared.

Holding his own breath, he became certain that he
heard someone else's breathing. They'd fooled him
again, he thought. He would have sworn that only two
of the gang had come through the broken glass, and
that two had also exited through the rear door. But
they'd tricked him somehow. One of them was still here,
waiting in ambush.

The breathing came from his left. Lyle turned his
head slowly, his eyes now well accustomed to the dark
and searching the room. For a moment, he thought that
perhaps there was nothing there; even the sound of the
breathing seemed to have stopped.

Had it all been imagination? No, those aroused instincts had been right. There was something there. But

because he couldn't see what it was, he waited. After a moment or so, the breathing came again, starting with a little poof of suddenly expelled air. He had to laugh, silently within himself. The guy hadn't been able to hold his breath indefinitely. He was no superman. He could be had.

With this realization came the opportunity. One of those infrequent cars coming down Majestic Avenue moved by now, its headlights poking into every window it passed. In the gleam of those lights, Lyle saw his new antagonist.

Standing flattened against a side wall. A hat, a topcoat, a gun in his fist. Lyle didn't hesitate. He'd been on the defensive all evening, and now at last he had a chance for revenge. He hurled the brick with all his might.

Mercifully perhaps—for Lyle Beckwith wasn't the sadistic kind—the headlights passed just as the brick sailed toward his target. Therefore Lyle did not see the damage he had wrought. He only heard the thud, the stifled cry, then another thud—that of a body hitting the floor.

After that he didn't linger. He squeezed out through the broken glass, found the street still empty. He started running again, this time toward his car. He didn't see any more men in topcoats and turned-down hats. He reached the car, unlocked it, got in and drove home.

There was nothing in the morning paper, but the afternoon edition was more enlightening. "Police Dragnet Catches Robber," the headline said.

"The police of our city," the story went on, "acted quickly and efficiently in the location and capture of a lone bandit. The bandit, a small man in a gray topcoat, appeared at the Majestic Pharmacy, 5021 Majestic Avenue, just before closing time at 10:00 P.M. He pointed a gun at the clerk, emptied the contents of the cash register into a briefcase, and fled on foot. The clerk, Richard Handy, telephoned a description of the bandit, and within less than five minutes plainclothes-

men from the Second District converged on the Majestic
Avenue area. After a chase of several blocks, during
which detectives fired five shots, the bandit was cornered
in Milo's haberdashery, 5234 Majestic. He had entered
the store by smashing a display window, but injured
himself. Detectives made the final capture inside the
haberdashery. The bandit, who has identified himself as
Roger Smith, is expected to recover from a fractured
skull, and is in Marlborough Hospital. The briefcase,
containing over six hundred dollars in cash, was re-
covered intact. . . ."

Lyle could easily reconstruct what had happened.
The bandit had been calmly walking away with the
loot when he heard the shots. So he'd found himself a
hiding place till the excitement died down. And he'd
been real cozy there, while he—poor innocent Lyle
Beckwith—had provided target practice for the law.
Reflecting on this, Lyle wasn't a bit sorry about his use
of the brick.

But his briefcase! The police have two briefcases. But
they're not mentioning that fact, are they? Because they
don't know how to explain it. Should he go down to the
Second District and claim his briefcase? He could easily
identify the lunch box and the thermos.

In the end, Lyle decided not to. The bandit had undoubtedly entered that store by forcing the rear door,
which explained his having found it ajar. That open
door was another puzzler for those cops, which they
weren't mentioning either. So it might be just like that
haberdasher Milo to charge Lyle for the broken window.
That would cost a bit more than his ten-dollar briefcase. Lyle's accountant's mind clicked. Charge it off—
ten bucks—to experience.

THE ALREADY DEAD

by C. B. Gilford

Joey Marven was sweating. Not just during daily practice in the stadium where sometimes fairly good-sized
crowds came to watch, nor just on Saturday afternoons
when he quarterbacked the team to one spectacular
victory after another—those were times of honest
sweat. Joey Marven was suffering from the big sweat,
the inside kind that drips out of the conscience and
isn't expelled by the pores, but accumulates, gnaws, and
rots away that thing called a man's integrity.

He wasn't cheating on exams. He didn't have to, he
was in the top third of his class. He wasn't stealing or
involved with gamblers. He didn't have to do that either.
With his athletic scholarship and his regular allow-
ance from home, he always had enough money.

But in quite another way, a more important way, he
was cheating, stealing, gambling; cheating on another
human being, stealing something more precious than
money from that other human being, gambling with
that other human being's future and happiness—a
woman, of course.

He was in a trap, and should have known that traps
don't open up by themselves and let the victim out.
The victim has to burst out. Violence aimed at something—somebody—is the only way. He should have
known. That was the way it was on the football field.

When you couldn't find a pass receiver, and the tacklers were overwhelming you, you burst out. But, of course, he didn't see that in the beginning, while the trap was closing.

He sneaked out to see Tris Kinnard on a Wednesday evening. He had realized he'd have to go back at least once more—not to start everything all over again, for he'd told her it was finished, and as far as he was concerned it was finished—but she'd taken his decision pretty hard, and he wanted to doublecheck on how she was getting along.

Her shift at the Red Carpet, he knew, ended at midnight, so he waited till past that time, then drove out to the edge of town, to that crummy old service station and general store. He parked in his usual place, well off the highway and under the trees, where his car was least likely to be noticed. Lights shone from a pair of second-story windows. She was home.

He eased out of the car, not forgetting to shut the door softly, walked across the empty gravel parking space, keeping to the shadows, and climbed the stairway at the rear of the building which led to her apartment. Familiar movements . . . familiar paths. He hesitated at the top of the steps, then knocked softly.

Suddenly he found himself smiling. He had never knocked at this door before. If he did it now, automatically, naturally, that meant he had accepted the fact that the love affair was finished.

There was no answer to his knock. Strange. He was certain that she was home. She might have left a light on in her absence, but not two lights. He knocked again, and waited.

When there was still no answer, he tried the knob. It turned easily. Opening the door, he walked in—and saw her instantly.

Joey Marven, the man with the quick reactions, as the sportswriters described him, couldn't move now. Tris Kinnard was in her tiny kitchen just off the living-room. Still wearing her waitress' uniform, she was kneeling in front of the open oven door, and her head was inside. The smell of gas was heavy, even at the door where Joey stood.

Nothing in Joey responded. His brain was as numb as his body. He could only stare at the horrible sight. The open door let in fresh air, but gas still poured from the oven. Was Tris unconscious? He couldn't tell from the position of her body. Or was she dead? The seconds ticked away while he stood motionless and did nothing.

Was he doing nothing because he wanted her dead?

That awful suspicion of himself roused him finally. He lunged into the kitchen, seized the girl by the waist, dragged her away from the stove, lifted her in his arms, and carried her out into the fresh air. His brain was functioning now. He hurried down the steps, laid his burden on the grass in a patch of moonlight. Trying to stay calm, he searched for a pulse. It was there, feeble, but it was there. Her breathing was shallow, but she was breathing.

He'd studied first aid. He knew the routine, so he knelt over her and began artificial respiration. The fresh air itself would revive her, he was sure, but he wanted to help her get more oxygen into her lungs. As he worked rhythmically, pressing on her rib cage, then letting go, his mind worked, too. He was taking a chance . . . he should call a doctor or get her to the hospital . . . but if he did, he would be involved . . . and that had to be avoided at almost any cost.

The gamble succeeded. When he stopped the artificial respiration, she was breathing easier. Her eyes remained closed, but her pulse was stronger too. She would live. The natural processes could take over now.

Joey raced back up the steps, entered the apartment holding a handkerchief over his nose and mouth, trying not to breathe. He turned off the gas, opened every window. The place had to be made habitable again. There was nowhere else to put the girl.

When he returned to Tris, he found her stirring, struggling back toward consciousness. Thinking she'd catch pneumonia lying there on the grass, he lifted her again and carried her to his car, let her lie prone on the front seat, both doors open.

Then he paced on the gravel for a while. An occasional car raced by on the highway, but apparently nobody noticed him or his car with its wide-flung doors. He checked the girl's condition every few minutes. She was improving, but he wanted to get her back upstairs as soon as possible.

Finally he went up himself. He walked all through the place, sniffed in all the corners. The smell of gas was still present but faint. The brisk night breeze had been clearing it out fast.

He sat down on the sofa, wondering if it were safe to bring Tris back up here yet. His eyes wandered for the first time to the little desk against the far wall. Among the litter there was a bright little white envelope. It was propped up against a penholder so that it would be very visible, but somehow he had failed to notice it. Her suicide note?

He rose from the sofa and approached the desk shakily. This wasn't good. He sensed it before he saw it. Then there it was, scrawled boldly on the face of the envelope. "Joey." He was trembling violently as he ripped the thing open.

"My dearest darling Joey," it read. "I will be dead when you read this, but what does it matter to you? I was already dead as far as you were concerned. You had found another girl. I guess I hope you will be happy with her. I'm not sure. All I am sure of is that I can't be happy without you. I can't face all those empty years ahead. I hope Alison Blair loves you as much as I do. But she couldn't. I don't think you love her. Do you know what love really is? Or are you just selfish and ambitious? Forgive me, Joey. I love you whatever you are. Goodbye. Tris."

He dropped the letter onto the desk, and it landed on a scattering of newspaper clippings. He recognized them because they matched his own collection. "Joey Marven leads State to victory . . . Joey Marven throws three TD passes . . . Joey Marven named 'back of the week' . . . Joey Marven likely to be State's first All-American in ten years . . ."

He turned away, put his face in his hands, trying to control the trembling that shook his whole body. Ye gods, it was all there on the desk! If he hadn't just happened to come by tonight, Tris would have been dead, and whoever found her would also have found all that stuff on the desk. It was all spelled out—for the police, for newspaper reporters, for everybody to see.

Joey Marven was already news, but on the sports page. Now he would have been on the front page. Girl commits suicide over football star . . . Alison Blair, daughter of tycoon Francis Simpson Blair, named in suicide note . . . dead waitress accuses Joey Marven of choosing ambition and money over real love . . . and on and on and on. The press would have a field day with big sports name Marven, and big business and society name Blair.

It would be the end of everything that he had just decided he wanted. The Blairs didn't mind publicity, but of the right sort, not the seamy sensational. He could just imagine old Frank's rage when his precious name was linked with a tawdry affair of a waitress gassing herself in a cheap apartment over the guy his own daughter was ready to marry. A daughter of the Blairs and an unknown waitress in the same triangle!

Joey staggered back to the sofa and sat there, shivering at the close call. He was too distracted to hear the sound of slow, dragging footsteps ascending the stairs outside. He wasn't prepared at all when Tris spoke to him from the open door.

"Joey . . ."

He spun to stare at her, not sure in the first moment whether it was Tris herself or whether Tris had died and this was her ghost come to haunt him. Her face was pale except for the dark hollows of her eyes. She'd always had a gaunt look, but now the thing that stared back at him seemed a skull dug out of a grave. Her hair, her long, glorious blonde hair, hung limply about the skull like the headpiece of a shroud.

"Joey," she asked, "why did you stop me?"

He had no answer. He stood up, confronting her as she leaned for support against the door jamb. Then when it seemed she was about to fall, he grabbed her, picked her up and carried her back to the small but neat bedroom.

There he deposited her on the bed gently, arranged her limp body so she would be comfortable, put a blanket over her because the crisp autumn night air was still blowing through the place. Her hair splayed out over the pillow. Her blue eyes, which seemed to have darkened almost to black, gazed up at him reproachfully.

"Why did you stop me, Joey?" she asked again.

He sat beside her on the edge of the bed. He felt groggy, confused. "Because what you were doing was crazy," he answered her.

She fingered the little charm she wore on a silver chain around her neck, a miniature football. It was the only gift he had ever given her, and she had never gone without it. "I love you, Joey. I don't want to live without you."

"That's crazy," he argued with her. "You're only nineteen, Tris. You'll get different ideas about a lot of things. You can't just decide to end it all now."

They talked on, covering the same ground they'd covered last Sunday night when he'd first told her it was finished between them. Sunday to Wednesday . . . in those three days she had changed from a beautiful young girl to a zombie. He grew desperate. He had to convince her. As he talked, he remembered how it all began, and wondered how, when it had begun so wonderfully, it could have come to this.

It had been his fault, because he had known Alison Blair, been almost engaged to marry her, before he met Tris Kinnard.

Alison had chased him all through the previous school

year, his junior year, because he had become a football star. He'd merely been flattered in the beginning, amused to have a wealthy girl chasing him. Then gradually he'd started to recognize the possibilities. His own parents were middle-class, and that was probably what he was condemned to be, but Alison was *rich*. She consorted with all the *best* people. When she took him home to meet her father, Francis Simpson Blair came right to the point.

"Are you and Alison serious?"

Joey remembered the conversation so clearly. "Well, not exactly, sir," he'd answered. "I mean . . . we have rather different backgrounds. . . ."

"You do that," the big man agreed, "but Alison seems serious. She brought you here to meet me, and despite your humility about your background, you had the guts to come here to meet me. Tell me, Mr. Marven, are you ambitious?"

"Yes, I am, sir."

"Are you ambitious in the direction of Blair Corporation?"

"Your company has an excellent reputation, sir."

"Yes, it does, and I've been thinking about how you might fit in. I didn't like the idea at first. I figured Alison was just impressed with your muscles, your glamour, your reputation, but then it occurred to me that your reputation just might fit into the corporation. You might be All-American next year. Then you might play pro ball. Well, that might be all right, too. The American public is very sports-conscious these days. They admire sports heroes. You might be a real asset to the corporation. And you happen to be pretty smart, too."

So Francis Simpson Blair had practically accepted him into the family. He still really wasn't engaged to Alison, but she always talked as if they'd get married after Joey's graduation. She probably would have preferred to make it sooner, but he'd held out for some reason.

He'd thought he knew what that reason was when at

the end of summer he'd gone off on that little one-
week vacation trip he'd wanted to take alone, and met
Tris Kinnard.

Then it all happened so quickly—love at first sight,
wild, wild passion—but more than that. It had been
beautiful at the same time; idyllic, nothing cheap or sordid about it, the most perfect week of his whole life.
Tris Kinnard was a magic girl—to him, anyway—but a
nobody.

He realized that fact, but he didn't think about it
during that week. She was a waitress there at that re-
sort, trying to earn a little money to start to college;
had left home because her parents quarreled. Not much
of a background, but a sweet girl, sweet and beautiful,
and he told her an hour after they'd met that he loved
her. Maybe he had.

Of course, she hadn't bothered with her waitress job
during that week. Time was suddenly precious, and they
spent every minute together. It was almost as if they
were on a honeymoon.

But then, of course, the week ended. It was time for
him to return to school . . . his senior year . . . early
football practice . . . a great season looming . . . maybe
All-American . . . graduation . . . Alison Blair . . . marriage . . . maybe a few years as a pro star . . . sand-
wiched in with Blair Corporation . . . and then the future . . . prosperity . . . wealth . . . importance . . .

So what was he to do with Tris Kinnard?

The alternatives were clear. Call it finished, walk off
and leave her, return to the university. Or, tell Alison
Blair he was in love with another girl, marry Tris Kinnard, say goodbye to Blair Corporation and all that
sweet deal.

Well, he didn't do either. He couldn't give up the al-
liance with the Blairs, and he couldn't give up Tris Kinnard, at least not quite yet.

Therefore, he compromised. That involved lying. He
told Tris an incredible pack of lies. He had to keep her
existence a secret, he told her. There was another girl—
he was partially truthful—from whom he had to get

disentangled, and that would take time. He had to keep strict training for football—partially truthful, too. He added for good measure that he had very conservative, straitlaced parents who lived just a few miles from the university. All these problems would have to be worked out. It would take time.

Tris wasn't to be dissuaded. She came to town, found herself a job and a place to live, remaining invisible and waiting patiently for the moments when he could sneak away. It was a beautiful arrangement for a few weeks. Their meetings had the added flavor of being secret, forbidden, infrequent, and therefore electric with the buildup of anticipation.

The pressure built up, too—studies, football, Alison —but worst of all his conscience. He was lying, cheating. He didn't intend to square everything so that he could marry Tris. Married to a waitress for the rest of his life? Condemned to middle-class mediocrity, held back by a wife who was lower than middle-class?

It was his conscience, not the fact that he was tired of her, that compelled him finally to say goodbye last Sunday night. "It just won't work," he had told her.

"It just won't work," he said again now to the pale form lying there on the bed.

"Yes, I realize that, Joey," she said. Her sad eyes looked up at him without life, without luster. "You've convinced me of that."

"All right then. You forget about me. You go somewhere else and find somebody new. There are plenty of guys. A girl like you can have her pick."

"I love you, Joey."

"You'll get over that."

She shook her head. "I'll love you forever. I don't want anybody else. All I want to do is die."

"No, you can't do that!"

How much more could he say to her? Did he dare tell her that, if she insisted on committing suicide, she could at least do it somewhere else, destroy those clippings, not write him a farewell note, leave him out of it completely? No, he couldn't give her instructions like that. She loved him, yes, and claimed to desire his happiness, but women were too unpredictable. Perhaps if he mentioned that involvement with her suicide would ruin him, it would be the very thing to cause her to trumpet his name to the world.

"You're going your way, Joey," she went on, "and I can't stop you. I have to go my way, too. My way is death. You can't stop me."

She meant it. Hadn't she already proved that she meant it?

Then the thought came to him. If she was absolutely determined to die, what difference would it make? What difference would it make if he were on the scene to keep his name out of it . . . and helped her to die?

So he had to pretend again, to lie and cheat again, and he did a good job. He told her he'd changed his mind about everything. Her suicide attempt had changed his mind. When he'd been afraid that she was dead and forever beyond his reach, he'd realized it was she whom he loved and wanted to marry, not Alison Blair.

She shouldn't have believed him, but she was confronted with such desperate alternatives—love or death —who could blame her for grasping frantically at the straw?

Tris remained home at her apartment through the weekend, not returning to her job, regaining her strength and equilibrium. Joey had a bad Saturday afternoon on the gridiron, almost losing the game with his erratic passing, and spent the last half on the bench. He was distracted, of course, not being able to give his full attention to football.

On Sunday he protested to Alison that he was still feeling glum about the game, and begged off from spending the day with her. Instead, he met Tris at a prearranged rendezvous along a side road a quarter of a mile from her apartment. Nobody saw her climb into his car.

"Where are we going?" she asked. She was radiant, beautiful again. Three days' rest and the reassurance of Joey's love had worked wonders.

"No place in particular," he answered. "Just thought we might spend the day together. Walk around in the fresh air. Then have dinner at some nice place."

"Oh, wonderful, Joey!" She clapped her hands, and then leaned across and kissed him on the cheek.

His skin burned under the touch of her lips. The kiss of Judas in reverse—the victim kissing the betrayer. He comforted his conscience with the inevitable logic of the situation. He couldn't marry her. No law said that he had to marry her, or be in love with her. If he didn't love and marry her, she would kill herself. He was only assisting a suicide. Yes, that was a crime, but it wasn't murder.

Joey appeared to be driving in random fashion, but he had the destination already picked out. He had been there before, not with Tris or Alison, but with another girl, long discarded. It had been a memorable afternoon with that other girl, so he remembered the place well. He had revisited the spot two days ago to check his memory and make detailed plans.

He had decided it would be safer to make the suicide appear as an accident, preferably an accident in which the body might not be discovered for a long time. He had considered and rejected a number of methods, including gas again, with his removing all evidences of himself later, but obvious suicide of any kind attracted publicity, and there was always the chance of a slipup. A quiet, private drowning was the method he chose. The mechanics were simpler, and it was something he could bring himself to do.

Tris wasn't aware of the distance and direction of their seemingly aimless wandering. They were nearly a hundred miles south of the campus when he eventually stopped the car well off a seldom-traveled country road in the midst of lonely hills and woods.

"Let's take a walk and scuff around in the leaves," he suggested.

His suggestion was a command to her. They went off hand in hand through the trees, although she stopped every now and then, flung herself into his arms, and kissed him passionately. She was feverishly gay, pulling him along deeper into the timber, initiating the embraces, chattering, laughing.

It was indeed a fine day for a hike in the woods. Some of the trees were losing their foliage, but most of it was still attached, brilliant yellows and reds and browns. The air was warm, and tangy with the smell of fallen leaves.

They came to the lake—not much more than a pond really—seemingly as a surprise. It nestled in a tiny valley, dark green and cold-looking amid all the warm colors. Tris was delighted. She let go of Joey's hand, ran down the hill alone in a swirl of flying leaves, and stood at the edge of the water enraptured.

"Isn't it lovely?" she called up to Joey.

He was checking the perimeter of hills and finding them empty of any human sign. He didn't know who the owner of this property might be, only that it was unfenced and probably useless except for the pond, and there was no house anywhere close by.

Joey joined Tris at the pond. She squeezed close to him, trembling with happiness.

"Joey, we're so alone here," she said.

Yes, he had planned that. His eyes were surveying the surface of the water, the banks, the hills around them once again. There was no one in sight, and still enough foliage on the trees to provide an effective screen.

"Oh, look," Tris said, "there's a rowboat." He knew, of course, that it was there, half-hidden beneath some overhanging branches. "Let's go for a ride, Joey."

He pretended to humor her. They untied the boat, pushed off, rowed to the middle of the pond, then drifted.

"Water looks inviting," he said after a few moments. He was impatient. The longer they stayed here, the more dangerous it was.

"You mean to swim, Joey?"

"Sure."

"You're crazy. It's ice-cold." She dipped her hand, pulled it back quickly.

"I don't care about that," he said.

She knew from the summer that he loved to swim. She couldn't swim a stroke, but she had been content to lie on the beach and watch him.

Joey rowed back to the bank, stepped out of the boat, and told Tris to row out to the middle again by herself. If the water proved too awful cold, he might want to climb aboard. Tris did as she was told. Remaining on the bank, Joey stripped down to his shorts, his eyes roaming the hills, still finding them empty. Then he plunged in.

The water was indeed cold, but he scarcely felt the shock. He swam to the boat, grinned up at Tris. She looked worried.

"Joey, you'll catch pneumonia."

In reply he dived down toward the bottom. It wasn't very far, perhaps eight feet. There was the usual muck down there, mud and rotted vegetation, but it was a smooth bottom, what he had hoped for, and what he needed. He came up gasping, and grabbed onto a gunwale of the boat, right amidships, where Tris was sitting.

"Joey, aren't you frozen?"

He looked up at her, debating for the last time. She wanted to die. If he left her, which he was going to do, she would take her own life. He wasn't committing murder, only being an accomplice to a suicide.

Then, after a final glance around the rim of hills, Joey pulled down mightily on the gunwale. Tris was too startled to utter a sound. The boat flipped over, and she joined him in the water.

It took a moment for him to find her. He merely wanted to make sure that she wasn't able to hang onto the boat. He discovered the boat was sinking too, and she was several feet away from it, thrashing about in the water, inexorably weighted down by her clothes.

Joey was prepared to push her under the surface

but, as he had hoped, he didn't have to. She was her
own efficient executioner. Her frantic efforts only exhausted her breath. She looked at him, a look of puzzlement, then of understanding. Once she understood,
she gave up the struggle. He wanted her to die, therefore she would die to satisfy his wish. She sank slowly,
as if some invisible hand were pulling her down.

He waited, treading water. He was alone now. Both
Tris and the boat had disappeared. Only a few bubbles
broke the smooth surface of the pond. Finally he dived.

He found her body quickly, towed it with him while
he searched for the boat. When he found it, there was
merely the matter of inserting the body beneath the
boat. That would keep the corpse there for a while, and,
if it were found, the inference would be clear: the girl
had drowned when the boat capsized. When he surfaced,
almost out of breath, the job was done.

He swam to the bank where he had left his clothes,
pulled the garments on over his wet, shivering body,
then walked back to the car. He saw no one on the
way.

That evening, he entered Tris' apartment with his
duplicate key, searched the place, and took away with
him all evidences of his connection with the dead girl.
When he left, he threw the key into the woods.

Except for two long-distance telephone conversations
with his parents, during which they expressed their
worry about last Saturday's game and Joey tried to re-
assure them, the week went by uneventfully until Friday.
Then the evening newspaper carried the story. A body
had been found.

The gruesome discovery had been made on wooded
land belonging to a farmer named Carl Finch. There
was a small lake or pond on Finch's property. Finch
kept a rowboat there, and he had found the oars float-
ing on the pond. Suspecting the boat had sunk, he had
grappled for it and found it. When the boat was re-
covered, a body floated up, the body of a girl.

That much would have been bad enough, but Finch
recognized the clothes the girl was wearing, because he

had *seen* that girl. The previous Sunday, he related, the girl came into Finch's woods accompanied by a man. "They were on my land, trespassing," Finch was quoted as saying, "but I didn't want to run them off because they looked like such a nice young couple, very romantic. I was up on top of a hill. I guess they didn't see me. I watched them for a while. They both looked very happy, especially the girl. She ran and skipped through the woods, and I could hear her laughing. They came to my pond, and the girl ran to it. Then she saw the boat, and it looked like she wanted to take a ride. So they both got into it together and rowed out to the middle of the pond. I didn't want to be a peeping tom, and it was dinnertime, so I left. I didn't see them after that."

Joey Marven almost fainted. It had been *that* close.

"The young man," Finch went on in the newspaper account, "is probably down there in the pond with her."

The authorities seemed to have agreed with Mr. Finch, for dragging operations had begun for the second body. Thus far none had been found. That seemed strange, because the pond was so small, a body should have been easy to locate within a matter of hours.

The dead girl had not as yet been identified, but the matter was being checked against lists of missing persons. Farmer Finch had not seen a car, nor had anyone else. It was being speculated that the couple might have been hiking, or had arrived in the neighborhood by bus, or been taken there in a third party's car. Still, the circumstance was suspicious, would continue to be until the second body was found.

Had Mr. Finch gotten a good look at the young man? Finch had never been close to the couple, but he claimed he had keen eyesight, and he would certainly recognize the young man if he saw him again.

Joey Marven was in a cold sweat when he put the newspaper down. He had a dinner date with Alison, and he decided to keep it, but he was a poor companion that evening, and he took Alison home early.

The next day, Saturday, was worse. He'd gotten very little sleep. He started the game at quarterback and played badly. He rode the bench most of the second half, and State barely squeaked by.

Joey found the Sunday paper interesting on two counts. The first concerned the story on the sports page. What had happened to Joey Marven? was the question asked. He had begun the season brilliantly, but had fallen apart in the last two games. The coach was angry and puzzled. Joey didn't seem to have his mind on football, he suggested.

The other story appeared on the front page. The lake on Carl Finch's property had been drained. There was no second body there. The state police and the local sheriff weren't sure yet, but they were coming to conclude now that the unidentified girl had been murdered.

Francis Simpson Blair was concerned enough about his prospective son-in-law to fly in for a visit. "What's the matter with you, Joey?" he demanded.

"I don't know exactly, sir."

"Well, look here now. You've got to find out what's the matter, and correct it. It isn't just a few football games we're talking about. You're going to build your career with Blair Corporation on your reputation as an athlete. That reputation is a solid business asset. It's got to be protected. I want it protected. Something's bothering you. What is it? Want to confide in me?"

"There's nothing to confide, sir."

"Maybe you should see a doctor. Maybe a psychiatrist."

"No, sir. Please, I'll be all right . . ."

Joey was Alison's property, too, and she was concerned. Alison was tall, slim, with a fashion-model look and a bony face. Last weekend she had been sympathetic, motherly. Now she was angry.

"People are asking me all the time," she told him, "what's wrong with you? It's gotten embarrassing. I'm having to avoid my best friends, and that just won't do."

"I'm sorry about that," he said.

"Do you realize the position you've put me in, Joey? Everything you do is news. Everybody knows about our relationship, so all of this bad publicity involves me, too."

"I'm sorry."

"Sorry! Is that all? What are you going to do about it?"

He was angry now, too. "Do you want to call it quits? Is that what you're telling me? Just tell me!"

"I didn't say that. I want you to snap out of it, that's all."

Snap out of it, that was all. He had killed a girl—or helped a girl kill herself—for her sake. And now she asked him to snap out of it.

"If you have any consideration at all for me, Joey, if you really want me, you'll have to snap out of it."

Next day the front page of the newspaper still reported on "The Girl in the Pond." An autopsy had confirmed the fact that she had indeed drowned, but there were no signs of struggle or violence.

What had happened? Police theorized that the drowning could have been an accident. Had her male escort simply become frightened and run away, afraid that he would be accused of murder? Why didn't he come forward now? Or had his relationship with the girl been a secret for some reason, and was he afraid to reveal that relationship?

A search for the young man was under way. Farmer Carl Finch had furnished a description. Clothes—gray sport jacket and trousers; not much help there. The physical description was better. Judging from his height when he was seen beside the girl, about six-two. Probably weighed about a hundred and ninety; broad-shouldered; close-cropped, dark brown hair; rather good-looking. Looked rather like an athlete, in fact—lithe, graceful, kind of rangy, probably a fast runner.

"I would guess," Carl Finch had said, "that he was of college age, and that if he goes to college, he's probably a football player. I'm a sports fan, especially football. I played a little at State years ago. This fellow maybe ought to be an end, or maybe a running back."

Joey stared at the words in the paper. He knew his own dimensions. He was six feet one and a half inches tall, and had weighed in last time at a hundred and ninety-two—and Finch had said he would recognize the girl's companion if he saw him again.

Joey started keeping the gray items of his wardrobe in the closet, and began wearing dark brown and blue.

At Wednesday's practice session the coach ran nothing but pass plays. Next Saturday's game was one of the toughest on the schedule. If anybody were going to snap State's victory string, the Wolves were the ones who might do it, and they would certainly do it if Joey Marven wasn't in top form. So, on Wednesday afternoon Joey threw a couple of hundred passes, and the coaching staff watched anxiously throughout his workout.

So did a sportswriter and his photographer who were allowed to watch the practice. Afterward, they begged for a brief interview with Joey Marven. The coach said he didn't mind.

"How's State going to do Saturday?" they asked Joey.

Joey hadn't had his mind on football very much that afternoon. Most of his passes had fallen into the arms of his receivers guided by experience and instinct, not by concentration, but he tried to pay attention now.

"We'll beat 'em," he answered automatically.

"You feel like you're in good shape, Joey?"

"Sure."

"Everybody knows you weren't up to par the last two games, Joey. How do you explain that?"

"All of us have our bad days."

It went on like that for a few minutes, eager questions and listless answers. Then the photographer interrupted, "How about a picture, Joey? No action thing this time, just stand there all sweaty and dirtied up. Shows you really worked hard today."

The man had raised his camera and aimed it at

Joey, close-up, almost on top of him. As the camera clicked, Joey's mind clicked, too . . . "I'm a sports fan, especially football . . . I'd recognize him if I saw him again. . . ."

Joey lunged, grabbed the camera, smashed it hard on the ground, then put his foot on it, pulverized it into twisted, useless metal with his heavy cleats.

"Hey, what are you doing?"

"No pictures. Just no pictures, see?"

Later, Alison cornered him. "Joey, I heard what you did to those reporters today." She was quivering with rage, her gaunt face aflame.

"I didn't want them to take pictures. I didn't say they could. Nobody said they could."

"You're a public figure!"

"I don't want to be a public figure."

She turned away, but the tautness in her shoulders and back was eloquent. "You're out of your mind these days," she said. "That's the only way I can describe you."

Yes, it was an accurate description. He was out of his mind. He had been for quite a while now.

Joey didn't want his face to appear in any newspaper that Carl Finch, football fan and State alumnus, might see, but his violence had the opposite effect from that which he'd desired.

The newspaper had a lot of pictures of Joey Marven on file. Vengefully now, they printed several, along with an account of Joey's encounter with the photographer. Two weeks ago Joey had been a hero both on the campus and in the town, but since he had dared to manhandle a journalist, he was fair game for bitter editorial gibes. In the process he received more publicity than ever before.

Desperate, he told the coach his decision on Friday. "Look, I won't be any good tomorrow. If you put me in at all, I'll just mess it up. I don't want to be there tomorrow. I'm resigning from the team."

Francis Simpson Blair had flown in to watch the game on Saturday. He and Alison finally cornered Joey in his dormitory room. The tycoon was better-controlled than his daughter. He was cold, rational, deadly.

"You've made an ugly situation for yourself, young man. The student body was with you against that newspaper, but if you don't show up at the stadium this afternoon, you'll be letting them down. They'll all consider that unforgivable. In one day, you'll lose all the admiration, all the good will, all the friendships you've built up here for four years. Nobody likes a quitter. All right, you've had some bad luck, you've been off your game. But you can't quit, not even if they grind you down in the dirt and walk all over you. The coach can take you out. But you can't quit!"

"Sir, I can't go out there today. . . ."

"Now, listen to me, boy. Is Alison important to you?"

"Yes."

"Is what I say important to you?"

"Yes."

"Is your future with the Blair family and Blair Corporation important to you?"

"Yes, it is."

"Then you get out there!"

"I can't do that, sir."

On Sunday morning, along with the sad tale of State's first defeat of the season, the newspaper reported that "The Girl in the Pond," whose body had been discovered almost a hundred miles away, had been identified as a resident of this university town. Her name was Tris Kinnard, and she had been a waitress at the Red Carpet.

The girl had lived alone in an apartment over a store and service station on the edge of town. The owner of the building had noticed a lack of any signs of occupancy, had entered the apartment with his own key. His description of his missing tenant had been eventually linked with the corpse a hundred miles south.

The building owner, a man named Klein, had made a rather positive identification. The bloated corpse itself was not recognizable, except for general dimensions and the color of the hair. What Mr. Klein did remember, however, was a small pendant or charm which she had always worn on a silver chain around her neck. The pendant was in the form of a tiny football.

Early Monday morning Joey consulted with his academic dean, and requested honorable withdrawal from the university. He might simply have run away, but his instinct for self-preservation, still functioning, told him that such a move would be too dramatic, would call too much attention to itself.

The dean was reluctant to accept withdrawal as the answer to Joey's problem. Like so many others, he counseled that Joey see a doctor, any kind of doctor. "After all," he said, "you didn't come here just to play football, Mr. Marven. You've been a very good student. The difficulty you've had on the athletic field shouldn't dissuade you from your primary goal of an education. As we all know, a man needs a college diploma these days."

"I'll have to do without it for the moment, sir. I just can't stay here."

The morning newspaper, which he purchased after leaving the dean's office, confirmed his fears. There was a long article on the front page concerning Tris Kinnard.

The situation was perfect for juicy speculation. The girl had been lured to a pond and drowned by a young man whom a witness had described as "looking like a football player." Her corpse had been identified because of the football charm on a necklace. The girl had arrived in town at the start of the school year—and, incidentally, the start of the football season.

Except for these clues, the girl's life was a mystery. Both her landlord and her employer stated that they had never seen her with any male escort, yet a girl like Tris Kinnard would surely have attracted masculine attention. She must have had a boyfriend, and he must have been the fellow who took her to the pond and drowned her, and he very likely was a student at

State. Not necessarily a football player, but there was always that possibility.

The local police would not go so far as to say they intended to question every member of the State football squad. They would, they announced, initiate an inquiry into Miss Kinnard's history, try to locate her relatives, try to discover where she had lived just previously to her arrival here, whom she might have known there, and therefore why she came to this university town when she did.

It was obvious enough to Joey Marven that somebody would soon connect two hitherto unrelated facts —Joey Marven had played his first bad football game on the day before Tris Kinnard died.

Joey drove south slowly, his mind a turmoil. He did not know precisely why he was driving in that direction.

To cover his tracks? It was rather late for that. Perhaps to confront that fellow Carl Finch, see if the man would recognize him, remember him—and if Finch could identify him, what then? Put Finch into the pond? He thought about it vaguely, not really considering or planning it, but just letting the possibility cavort in his imagination.

The miles ticked off, as if some relentless magnet were pulling him. He turned off onto the familiar side road, parked in the same place where he had parked before.

Now there was a change, he noted, in the hills and woods. The trees were almost bare. The earth, which had displayed some green before, was now brown with a thick carpet of fallen leaves. The bright colors of autumn had given way to the desolation of approaching winter. There was a frosty bite in the air. The season of death was here.

He walked, certain that he was following the exact route that he had taken before, his feet treading on the imprints they had made at that other time. He could see those imprints stretching out ahead of him, marking the path he must take, and remorselessly his body, his legs, moved him along it.

No, there was a double path, two sets of prints parallel to each other; one for himself, one for Tris. He glanced sideways, and he saw her there. She was laughing, chattering, desperately gay. She took his hand and pulled him along the double path. Her hand was warm, almost hot, but he could not withdraw his own from its grasp. She was beautiful, her blonde hair flying, her eyes sparkling, her lips parting as she laughed.

"I am going to marry Alison Blair," he told her.

She didn't hear him. She only pulled him farther into the woods.

"Of course," he added, "I'm in love with you. I really don't feel anything the same about Alison. I don't even like her really, and she doesn't like me, only the idea that I'm a famous football star. The minute I stop being that, she won't have any feeling toward me at all. And her old man . . . to him I'm only an asset, worth a certain amount of money to his corporation, but I've got to think about my future, you see. That's why I'm going to marry Alison. But I'll always be in love with you, Tris."

They came at last to the lake.

"I thought they'd drained it," he said.

They must have repaired the dam though, and then there must have been rain. Yes, rain—there was a dampness in the leaves underfoot—and it wasn't a very big lake.

Tris had let go of his hand, and had gone running down the hill. She stopped at the edge of the lake and stood gazing at it.

"Isn't it lovely?" she called back to him.

He looked around at the perimeter of hills. The trees were bare now. He should have been able to see Mr. Finch, but he couldn't. The man was there, he knew, watching. Mr. Finch would be watching. "They looked like such a nice young couple, very romantic." Yes, Mr. Finch was always watching.

He joined Tris at the edge of the little lake. "Oh

look," she said, "there's a rowboat. Let's go for a ride, Joey."

Of course, he would take her for a ride. He loved her, he wanted to please her. He loved Tris. Why couldn't he always have remembered that? So he untied the boat, and they rowed out to the middle of the pond, where they drifted.

"Water looks inviting," he said.

"You mean to swim, Joey?"

"Sure."

"You're crazy. It's ice-cold."

He rowed back to the bank anyway. He was a swimmer, and if you were a swimmer, you swam. Tris rowed the boat out into the middle again, and he stripped down to his shorts and plunged in.

"Joey, you'll catch pneumonia. Aren't you frozen?"

The water was his natural element. He belonged there. "I love to swim," he told her.

"You go your way, Joey," she answered, "but I have to go my way, too. My way is death."

"No, you can't do that!"

"You can't stop me. I'll love you forever. All I want to do is die."

Because he loved her, it was up to him to help her if she wanted to die—as an accomplice to her suicide, not as a murderer.

He reached up, grabbed a gunwale, and flipped the boat over. Then she was there in the water beside him. She looked at him, first in puzzlement, then in understanding. He wanted her to die, therefore she would die to satisfy his wish. Slowly she sank.

"I love you, Tris!" he shouted after her. "Don't leave me!" Then he dived. After a frantic search he found her. "I love you, Tris," he whispered, embracing her, letting her blonde hair, her mermaid's hair, swirl about his face. "You're the one I love. I've decided that now."

Taking her with him, he found the sunken rowboat, and crawled under it. Now there would be two bodies, as there always should have been.

#8

by Jack Ritchie

I was doing about eighty, but the long, flat road made it feel only half that fast.

The redheaded kid's eyes were bright and a little wild as he listened to the car radio. When the news bulletin was over, he turned down the volume.

He wiped the side of his mouth with his hand. "So far they found seven of his victims."

I nodded. "I was listening." I took one hand off the wheel and rubbed the back of my neck, trying to work out some of the tightness.

He watched me and his grin was half-sly. "You nervous about something?"

My eyes flicked in his direction. "No. Why should I be?"

The kid kept smiling. "The police got all the roads blocked for fifty miles around Edmonton."

"I heard that, too."

The kid almost giggled. "He's too smart for them."

I glanced at the zipper bag he held on his lap. "Going far?"

He shrugged. "I don't know."

The kid was a little shorter than average and he had a slight build. He looked about seventeen, but he was the baby-face type and could have been five years older.

He rubbed his palms on his slacks. "Did you ever wonder what made him do it?"

I kept my eyes on the road. "No."

He licked his lips. "Maybe he got pushed too far. All his life somebody always pushed him. Somebody was always there to tell him what to do and what not to do. He got pushed once too often."

The kid stared ahead. "He exploded. A guy can take just so much. Then something's got to give."

I eased my foot on the accelerator.

He looked at me. "What are you slowing down for?"

"Low on gas," I said. "The station ahead is the first I've seen in the last forty miles. It might be another forty before I see another."

I turned off the road and pulled to a stop next to the three pumps. An elderly man came around to the driver's side of the car.

"Fill the tank," I said. "And check the oil."

The kid studied the gas station. It was a small building, the only structure in the ocean of wheat fields. The windows were grimy with dust.

I could just make out a wall phone inside.

The kid jiggled one foot. "That old man takes a long time. I don't like waiting." He watched him lift the hood to check the oil. "Why does anybody that old want to live? He'd be better off dead."

I lit a cigarette. "He wouldn't agree with you."

The kid's eyes went back to the filling station. He grinned. "There's a phone in there. You want to call anybody?"

I exhaled a puff of cigarette smoke. "No."

When the old man came back with my change, the kid leaned toward the window. "You got a radio, mister?"

The old man shook his head. "No. I like things quiet."

The kid grinned. "You got the right idea, mister. When things are quiet, you live longer."

Out on the road, I brought the speed back up to eighty.

The kid was quiet for a while, and then he said, "It took guts to kill seven people. Did you ever hold a gun in your hand?"

"I guess almost everybody has."

His teeth showed through twitching lips. "Did you ever point it at anybody?"

I glanced at him.

His eyes were bright. "It's good to have people afraid of you," he said. "You're not short any more when you got a gun."

"No," I said. "You're not a runt any more."

He flushed slightly.

"You're the tallest man in the world," I said. "As long as nobody else has a gun, too."

"It takes a lot of guts to kill," the kid said again. "Most people don't know that."

"One of those killed was a boy of five," I said. "You got anything to say about that?"

He licked his lips. "It could have been an accident."

I shook my head. "Nobody's going to think that."

His eyes seemed uncertain for a moment. "Why do you think he'd kill a kid?"

I shrugged. "That would be hard to say. He killed one person and then another and then another. Maybe after awhile it didn't make any difference to him what they were. Men, women, or children. They were all the same."

The kid nodded. "You can develop a taste for killing. It's not too hard. After the first few, it doesn't matter. You get to like it."

He was silent for another five minutes. "They'll never get him. He's too smart for that."

I took my eyes off the road for a few moments. "How do you figure that? The whole country's looking for him. Everybody knows what he looks like."

The kid lifted both his thin shoulders. "Maybe he doesn't care. He did what he had to do. People will know he's a big man now."

We covered a mile without a word and then he

shifted in his seat. "You heard his description over the radio?"

"Sure," I said. "For the last week."

He looked at me curiously. "And you weren't afraid to pick me up?"

"No."

His smile was still sly. "You got nerves of steel?"

I shook my head. "No. I can be scared when I have to, all right."

He kept his eyes on me. "I fit the description perfectly."

"That's right."

The road stretched ahead of us and on both sides there was nothing but the flat plain. Not a house. Not a tree.

The kid giggled. "I look just like the killer. Everybody's scared of me. I like that."

"I hope you had fun," I said.

"I been picked up by the cops three times on this road in the last two days. I get as much publicity as the killer."

"I know," I said. "And I think you'll get more. I thought I'd find you somewhere on this highway."

I slowed down the car. "How about me? Don't I fit the description, too?"

The kid almost sneered. "No. You got brown hair. His is red. Like mine."

I smiled. "But I could have dyed it."

The kid's eyes got wide when he knew what was going to happen.

He was going to be number eight.

THE DAY OF
THE EXECUTION

by Henry Slesar

When the jury foreman stood up and read the verdict, Warren Selvey, the prosecuting attorney, listened to the pronouncement of guilt as if the words were a personal citation of merit. He heard in the foreman's somber tones, not a condemnation of the accused man who shriveled like a burnt match on the courtroom chair, but a tribute to Selvey's own brilliance. *"Guilty as charged . . ."* No, Warren Selvey thought triumphantly, guilty as I've proved . . .

For a moment, the judge's melancholy eye caught Selvey's and the old man on the bench showed shock at the light of rejoicing that he saw there. But Selvey couldn't conceal his flush of happiness, his satisfaction with his own efforts, with his first major conviction.

He gathered up his documents briskly, fighting to keep his mouth appropriately grim, though it ached to smile all over his thin, brown face. He put his briefcase beneath his arm, and when he turned, faced the buzzing spectators. "Excuse me," he said soberly, and pushed his way through to the exit doors, thinking now only of Doreen.

He tried to visualize her face, tried to see the red mouth that could be hard or meltingly soft, depending on which one of her many moods happened to be dominant. He tried to imagine how she would look when she heard his good news, how her warm body would feel against his, how her arms would encompass him.

But this imagined foretaste of Doreen's delights was interrupted. There were men's eyes seeking his now, and men's hands reaching toward him to grip his hand in congratulation. Garson, the district attorney, smiling heavily and nodding his lion's head in approval of his cub's behavior. Vance, the assistant D.A., grinning with half a mouth, not altogether pleased to see his junior in the spotlight. Reporters, too, and photographers, asking for statements, requesting poses.

Once, all this would have been enough for Warren Selvey. This moment, and these admiring men. But now there was Doreen, too, and thought of her made him eager to leave the arena of his victory for a quieter, more satisfying reward.

But he didn't make good his escape. Garson caught his arm and steered him into the gray car that waited at the curb.

"How's it feel?" Garson grinned, thumping Selvey's knee as they drove off.

"Feels pretty good," Selvey said mildly, trying for the appearance of modesty. "But, hell, I can't take all the glory, Gar. Your boys made the conviction."

"You don't really mean that." Garson's eyes twinkled. "I watched you through the trial, Warren. You were tasting blood. You were an avenging sword. You put him on the waiting list for the chair, not me."

"Don't say that!" Selvey said sharply. "He was guilty as sin, and you know it. Why, the evidence was clearcut. The jury did the only thing it could."

"That's right. The way you handled things, they did the only thing they could. But let's face it, Warren. With another prosecutor, maybe they would have done something else. Credit where credit's due, Warren."

Selvey couldn't hold back the smile any longer. It illumined his long, sharp-chinned face, and he felt the relief of having it relax his features. He leaned back against the thick cushion of the car.

"Maybe so," he said. "But I thought he was guilty, and I tried to convince everybody else. It's not just A-B-C evidence that counts, Gar. That's law-school sophistry, you know that. Sometimes you just *feel . . .*"

"Sure." The D.A. looked out of the window. "How's the bride, Warren?"

"Oh, Doreen's fine."

"Glad to hear it. Lovely woman, Doreen."

She was lying on the couch when he entered the apartment. He hadn't imagined this detail of his triumphant homecoming.

He came over to her and she shifted slightly on the couch to let his arms surround her.

He said: "Did you hear, Doreen? Did you hear what happened?"

"I heard it on the radio."

"Well? Don't you know what it means? I've got my conviction. My first conviction, and a big one. I'm no junior anymore, Doreen."

"What will they do to that man?"

He blinked at her, tried to determine what her mood might be. "I asked for the death penalty," he said. "He killed his wife in cold blood. Why should he get anything else?"

"I just asked, Warren." She put her cheek against his shoulder.

"Death is part of the job," he said. "You know that as well as I do, Doreen. You're not holding that against me?"

She pushed him away for a moment, appeared to be deciding whether to be angry or not. Then she drew him quickly to her, her breath hot and rapid in his ear.

They embarked on a week of celebration. Quiet, intimate celebration, in dim supper clubs and with close acquaintances. It wouldn't do for Selvey to appear publicly gay under the circumstances.

On the evening of the day the convicted Murray Rodman was sentenced to death, they stayed at home and drank hand-warmed brandy from big glasses.

Doreen got drunk and playfully passionate, and Selvey thought he could never be happier. He had parlayed a mediocre law-school record and an appointment as a third-class member of the state legal department into a position of importance and respect. He had married a beautiful, pampered woman and could make her whimper in his arms. He was proud of himself. He was grateful for the opportunity Murray Rodman had given him.

It was on the day of Rodman's scheduled execution that Selvey was approached by the stooped, gray-haired man with the grease-spotted hat.

He stepped out of the doorway of a drugstore, his hands shoved into the pockets of his dirty tweed overcoat, his hat low over his eyes. He had white stubble on his face.

"Please," he said. "Can I talk to you a minute?"

Selvey looked him over, and put a hand in his pocket for change.

"No," the man said quickly. "I don't want a handout. I just want to talk to you, Mr. Selvey."

"You know who I am?"

"Yeah, sure, Mr. Selvey. I read all about you."

Selvey's hard glance softened. "Well, I'm kind of rushed right now. Got an appointment."

"This is important, Mr. Selvey. Honest to God. Can't we go someplace? Have coffee maybe? Five minutes is all."

"Why don't you drop me a letter, or come down to the office? We're on Chambers Street—"

"It's about that man, Mr. Selvey. The one they're executing tonight."

The attorney examined the man's eyes. He saw how intent and penetrating they were.

"All right," he said. "There's a coffee shop down the street. But only five minutes, mind you."

It was almost two-thirty; the lunchtime rush at the coffee shop was over. They found a booth in the rear, and sat silently while a waiter cleared the remnants of a hasty meal from the table.

Finally, the old man leaned forward and said: "My

name's Arlington, Phil Arlington. I've been out of town, in Florida, else I wouldn't have let things go this far. I didn't see a paper, hear a radio, nothing like that."

"I don't get you, Mr. Arlington. Are you talking about the Rodman trial?"

"Yeah, the Rodman business. When I came back and heard what happened, I didn't know what to do. You can see that, can't you? It hurt me, hurt me bad to read what was happening to that poor man. But I was afraid. You can understand that. I was afraid."

"Afraid of what?"

The man talked to his coffee. "I had an awful time with myself, trying to decide what to do. But then I figured—hell, this Rodman is a young man. What is he, thirty-eight? I'm sixty-four, Mr. Selvey. Which is better?"

"Better for what?" Selvey was getting annoyed; he shot a look at his watch. "Talk sense, Mr. Arlington. I'm a busy man."

"I thought I'd ask your advice." The gray-haired man licked his lips. "I was afraid to go to the police right off, I thought I should ask you. Should I tell them what I did, Mr. Selvey? Should I tell them I killed that woman? Tell me. Should I?"

The world suddenly shifted on its axis. Warren Selvey's hands grew cold around the coffee cup. He stared at the man across from him.

"What are you talking about?" he said. "Rodman killed his wife. We proved that."

"No, no, that's the point. I was hitchhiking east. I got a lift into Wilford. I was walking around town, trying to figure out where to get food, a job, anything. I knocked on this door. This nice lady answered. She didn't have no job, but she gave me a sandwich. It was a ham sandwich."

"What house? How do you know it was Mrs. Rodman's house?"

"I know it was. I seen her picture, in the newspapers. She was a nice lady. If she hadn't walked into that kitchen after, it would have been okay."

"What, what?" Selvey snapped.

"I shouldn't have done it. I mean, she was real nice to me, but I was so broke. I was looking around the jars in the cupboard. You know how women are; they're always hiding dough in the jars, house money they call it. She caught me at it and got mad. She didn't yell or anything, but I could see she meant trouble. That's when I did it, Mr. Selvey. I went off my head."

"I don't believe you," Selvey said. "Nobody saw any—anybody in the neighborhood. Rodman and his wife quarreled all the time—"

The gray-haired man shrugged. "I wouldn't know anything about that, Mr. Selvey. I don't know anything about those people. But that's what happened, and that's why I want your advice." He rubbed his forehead. "I mean, if I confess now, what would they do to me?"

"Burn you," Selvey said coldly. "Burn you instead of Rodman. Is that what you want?"

Arlington paled. "No. Prison, okay. But not that."

"Then just forget about it. Understand me, Mr. Arlington? I think you dreamed the whole thing, don't you? Just think of it that way. A bad dream. Now get back on the road and forget it."

"But that man. They're killing him tonight—"

"Because he's guilty." Selvey's palm hit the table. "I *proved* him guilty. Understand?"

The man's lip trembled.

"Yes, sir," he said.

Selvey got up and tossed a five on the table.

"Pay the bill," he said curtly. "Keep the change."

That night, Doreen asked him the hour for the fourth time.

"Eleven," he said sullenly.

"Just another hour." She sank deep into the sofa cushions. "I wonder how he feels right now. . . ."

"Cut it out!"

"My, we're jumpy tonight."

"My part's done with, Doreen. I told you that again and again. Now the State's doing its job."

She held the tip of her pink tongue between her teeth thoughtfully. "But you put him where he is, Warren. You can't deny that."

"The jury put him there!"

"You don't have to shout at *me,* attorney."

"Oh, Doreen . . ." He leaned across to make some apologetic gesture, but the telephone rang.

He picked it up angrily.

"Mr. Selvey? This is Arlington."

All over Selvey's body, a pulse throbbed.

"What do you want?"

"Mr. Selvey, I been thinking it over. What you told me today. Only I don't think it would be right, just forgetting about it. I mean——"

"Arlington, listen to me. I'd like to see you at my apartment. I'd like to see you right now."

From the sofa, Doreen said: "Hey!"

"Did you hear me, Arlington? Before you do anything rash, I want to talk to you, tell you where you stand legally. I think you owe that to yourself."

There was a pause at the other end.

"Guess maybe you're right, Mr. Selvey. Only I'm way downtown, and by the time I get there——"

"You can make it. Take the IRT subway, it's quickest. Get off at 86th Street."

When he hung up, Doreen was standing.

"Doreen, wait. I'm sorry about this. This man is—— an important witness in a case I'm handling. The only time I can see him is now."

"Have fun," she said airily, and went to the bedroom.

"Doreen——"

The door closed behind her. For a moment, there was silence. Then she clicked the lock.

Selvey cursed his wife's moods beneath his breath, and stalked over to the bar.

By the time Arlington sounded the door chimes, Selvey had downed six inches of bourbon.

Arlington's grease-spotted hat and dirty coat looked worse than ever in the plush apartment. He took them off and looked around timidly.

"We've only got three-quarters of an hour," he said. "I've just got to do something, Mr. Selvey."

"I know what you can do," the attorney smiled. "You can have a drink and talk things over."

"I don't think I should—" But the man's eyes were already fixed on the bottle in Selvey's hands. The lawyer's smile widened.

By eleven-thirty, Arlington's voice was thick and blurred, his eyes no longer so intense, his concern over Rodman no longer so compelling.

Selvey kept his visitor's glass filled.

The old man began to mutter. He muttered about his childhood, about some past respectability, and inveighed a string of strangers who had done him dirt. After awhile, his shaggy head began to roll on his shoulders, and his heavy-lidded eyes began to close.

He was jarred out of his doze by the mantel clock's chiming.

"Whazzat?"

"Only the clock," Selvey grinned.

"Clock? What time? What time?"

"Twelve, Mr. Arlington. Your worries are over. Mr. Rodman's already paid for his crime."

"No!" The old man stood up, circling wildly. "No, that's not true. I killed that woman. Not him! They can't kill him for something he—"

"Relax, Mr. Arlington. Nothing you can do about it now."

"Yes, yes! Must tell them—the police—"

"But why? Rodman's been executed. As soon as that clock struck, he was dead. What good can you do him now?"

"Have to!" the old man sobbed. "Don't you see? Couldn't live with myself, Mr. Selvey. Please—"

He tottered over to the telephone. Swiftly the attorney put his hand on the receiver.

"Don't," he said.

Their hands fought for the instrument, and the younger man's won easily.

"You won't stop me, Mr. Selvey. I'll go down there myself. I'll tell them all about it. And I'll tell them about you—"

He staggered toward the door. Selvey's arm went out and spun him around.

"You crazy old tramp! You're just asking for trouble. Rodman's dead—"

"I don't care!"

Selvey's arm lashed out and his hand cracked across the sagging, white-whiskered face. The old man sobbed at the blow, but persisted in his attempt to reach the door. Selvey's anger increased and he struck out again, and after the blow, his hands dropped to the old man's scrawny neck. The next idea came naturally. There wasn't much life throbbing in the old throat. A little pressure, and Selvey could stop the frantic breathing, the hoarse, scratchy voice, the damning words . . .

Selvey squeezed, harder and harder.

And then his hands let him go. The old man swayed and slid against Selvey's body to the floor.

In the doorway, rigid, icy-eyed: Doreen.

"Doreen, listen—"

"You choked him," she said.

"Self-defense!" Selvey shouted. "He broke in here, tried to rob the apartment."

She slammed the door shut, twisted the inside lock. Selvey raced across the carpet and pounded desperately on the door. He rattled the knob and called her name, but there was no answer. Then he heard the sound of a spinning telephone dial.

It was bad enough, without having Vance in the crowd that jammed the apartment. Vance, the assistant D.A., who hated his guts anyway. Vance, who was smart enough to break down his burglar story without any trouble, who had learned that Selvey's visitor had been expected. Vance, who would delight in his predicament.

But Vance didn't seem delighted. He looked puzzled. He stared down at the dead body on the floor of Selvey's apartment and said: "I don't get it, Warren. I just don't get it. What did you want to kill a harmless old guy like that for?"

"Harmless? *Harmless?*"

"Sure. Harmless. That's old Arlington, I'd know him any place."

"You know him?" Selvey was stunned.

"Sure, I met up with him when I was working out of Bellaire County. Crazy old guy goes around confessing to murders. But why kill him, Warren? What for?"

WHO HAS BEEN SITTING IN MY CHAIR?

by Helen Nielsen

When Eddie Wanamaker walked through the prison gates, he knew Hilda would be waiting. She hadn't missed a visiting day during the entire year he'd served for manslaughter, which, in Eddie's case, was legal terminology for killing a man with an automobile he couldn't remember driving on a night when he'd certainly been somewhere else.

"Honey—"

Hilda's arms about his neck, and her mouth on his, blotted out the bitterness for one wonderful moment. It was the first time in a year that Eddie had felt the warm promise of a living kiss, and for that moment it was as if nothing had happened at all.

But it had happened. As the kiss ended, Eddie remembered. He crawled into the front seat of the Ford next to Hilda.

"I packed your camping clothes and fishing gear in the trunk," she said. "The trout season opened at Indian Gorge last week."

"I'd rather go home," Eddie said.

"But the trout—"

"I want to get started. I've had a whole year to think about it; now I'm going to do something about it."

Hilda was pretty. Six years married to Eddie Wanamaker, and she still looked like a photograph in the Emerald City High School Year Book. Her hair was blonde—always a little sun-streaked because she liked to drive the Ford with the top down; her eyes were gray, and her chin was just like Grandfather Huston's in Dr. Huston's front office, where he had proposed to her the first time. But she was afraid, and he was going to have to make her more afraid.

"Please, Eddie, it's all over now. Let it die."

"I've served a year in prison," Eddie said.

"But nobody blames you for what happened. Daddy doesn't, and Paul's waiting for you to come back to work. Please try to forget."

"Forget!" Eddie repeated bitterly. "My name is Eddie Wanamaker. Up until a year ago, it was a good name. I'd worked hard to make it a good name. I won't rest until I've made it a good name again."

He looked at her for reassurance, but all he could see was the fear in her eyes. Suddenly, he knew what he'd fought knowing for a long, cold year.

"You think I really did drive that car," he said.

"I think that I love you, Eddie, and I don't want you to be hurt any more."

She had denied nothing. The cold year lay between them like an invisible wall, and there was only one way to tear it down.

"Let's get going," he said. "If we start now, we can be home by dark."

Emerald City. It had been adobe dust and scrub brush, with the sun and wind conspiring to make a desolation just short of the nether world, until the army decided it was an ideal location for an air training base. Subsequently, the base had converted to missiles, and the adobe had blossomed forth with a city of over 20,000 hardy souls, the greater portion of whom were under 35 and enthusiastically reproducing.

Seven years ago, with the population growing rapidly even then, Eddie had descended from the bus at the city terminal with his total assets contained within his leather Air Force jacket and tans. He had a shock of coppery red hair, a frank, clean-shaven face, and no next of kin. He also had a piece of North Korean flack in one shoulder, and an honorable discharge in his pocket. He'd come to Emerald City for two reasons: firstly, he had no place to go; secondly, he'd fallen off a curb and sprained his ankle on Main Street one day two years previous and been treated in Dr. Huston's office by the loveliest girl he'd ever seen. Eddie was a timid sort of guy; but the uniform, the sprain, and the two beers he'd consumed before the fall, had given him the courage to ask her for a date. Three days later, he had asked her to marry him.

"When I get out of high school," Hilda had said, "and you get out of the service, come back and see me again."

Two years later, Eddie returned. This time he had no beers to fortify his nerve, and the whole idea seemed a little wild. But Eddie had been looking for a place to come home to since he'd run away from an orphanage at the age of twelve, and Hilda and Emerald City was the dream he'd carried with him all through Korea.

He had found her behind the reception desk in Dr. Huston's office, but she wasn't alone. A good-looking young man about ten years Eddie's senior was perched on the edge of the desk engaged in a conversation that seemed to be highly unprofessional. Eddie started to back out, but that was when the first miracle of his life occurred. Hilda had looked up, stared, and then smiled in bright recognition.

"It's Eddie! It's Eddie Wanamaker!" she exclaimed. "You've come back!"

All the way from the bus station, Eddie had rehearsed a brilliant and witty entrance speech. Now he delivered it.

"Hi," he said.

"Paul—this is Eddie Wanamaker."

Paul was Paul Fenton, who got up from the desk and gripped Eddie's hand like a lodge brother. There was the standard greeting for a stranger returned, and then questions: How long was he staying? What were his plans? Eddie never took his eyes off Hilda when he answered. He'd like to stay if he could find a job. He didn't know what he could do, besides being a tail gunner. That was when Paul had flashed the lame duck on his lapel—token of a previous war—and offered him a job as salesman with his company.

"All you need is drive and personality," he explained. "The product sells itself."

"What product?" Eddie asked.

"Emerald City," Paul said. "Here's my card. The office is just down the street. Drop in tomorrow and we'll talk terms. As for you, young lady"—Paul had given Hilda a look that made Eddie jealous—"I'll pick you up at seven-thirty. Don't be late now. I'm nervous enough already."

Paul left the office hurriedly. In time, Eddie would learn that Paul was always in a hurry; but at the moment he was almost afraid to ask the reason. There was one particular appointment that made any man nervous; but did people get married at seven-thirty?

"It's the One Hundred Sons," Hilda explained. "The One Hundred leading business and professional men in Emerald City. They're having their annual dinner tonight. Daddy's the past chairman, and tonight Paul is being installed for the next term."

The social set. Eddie suddenly felt very shabby in his old Air Force jacket and tans.

"Well, I guess I'll move on and get the lay of the place," Eddie had said. "You know how it is. You remember a town and think it's great, and then you come back and it's just another town. I may not stay after all."

And that was when the second miracle in Eddie's life occurred. "I want you to stay, Eddie," Hilda said.

That night Eddie had taken a walk down a Main Street that was as dark and empty as any other Main Street—except for one thing.

"I want you to stay, Eddie."

"Okay," Eddie had said aloud. "I'm staying. Do you hear that, Emerald City? My name is Eddie Wanamaker, and I'm staying right here in this town!"

That had been seven years ago.

Driving back from the prison, Hilda came down Main Street very slowly. It was late and all the business houses were closed, but Hilda drove directly to Paul's office and stopped long enough for him to see the new lettering on the window: Fenton and Wanamaker, Land Development Co.

Fenton and Wanamaker. A year earlier, Eddie would have had Hilda stop the car so he could get out and do handsprings on the sidewalk; but now he could only read his name on the window with a sense of suspicion that had grown so luxuriously in a cell with an iron-grill door.

Is that how he buys off his conscience? Eddie thought.

Aloud, he said, "Okay, I've seen it. Let's go home."

Sam Nickols had died quickly. That was the one thing everyone had been grateful for—even his wife and their two children. The heavy fenders of Dr. Huston's Cadillac, traveling at an estimated speed of seventy miles an hour, had thrown Sam almost twenty feet from the point of contact and hurled him, head first, against a fire hydrant near the corner of Main and Joshua. Six blocks further down Main Street, after traveling in what two eye-witnesses described as a "wild, drunken manner," Dr. Huston's Cadillac had piled up against a lamp post and there, too intoxicated to know where he was, or to remember how he'd gotten there, was where the police had found Eddie slumped over the steering wheel. He was in a dazed condition; but at the emergency hospital where he was taken for treatment, the only injury found was a cut of unknown origin on the back of his head just above the left ear. The attending physician had removed a fragment of green bottle glass from the wound, of which Eddie's lawyer made much at the trial. Eddie Wanamaker couldn't hold liquor—all who knew him socially were aware of that. But he had been drinking; the evidence was on his breath and in his blood stream when he was arrested. Where he'd done the drinking no one had been able to ascertain; but Eddie's defense contended that it was at some place where violence had occurred.

This was the crux of his defense. A citizen of good standing in the community, it was unthinkable that he would have taken his father-in-law's automobile in a surreptitious manner—unwiring the extra ignition key from under the rear bumper where he knew Dr. Huston kept it—when all he had to do was make an open request for the use of the vehicle. He was an injured man when he'd taken the car—that was the story. A dazed man—not just another drunk. The jury had listened and the jury had believed to the extent of a light sentence; but Eddie had never remembered the scene of violence, or taking Dr. Huston's car, or even hitting Sam Nickols. It seemed that even a drunken man should remember something that important.

The next day, after Eddie's return to Emerald City, was Sunday. Exhausted after the long drive, Hilda slept late; but Eddie had work to do. Sam Nickols had lived in one of the old prewar houses over on East Fourth Street. It was probably paid for—Sam had been the only plumbing contractor in town up until five years ago. His widow, even with two children, wouldn't have been left destitute. But just to make sure that he didn't barge in on strangers, Eddie consulted the Emerald City telephone directory and found, to his surprise, that Mrs. Sam Nickols was listed at an address on Mustang Road. That was in the new Desert Vista section, a development Paul had in the surveying stage when Sam collided with sudden death. Eddie left Hilda sleeping and went to the car.

Desert Vista had grown far beyond the surveying stage. Mustang Road was totally built up; the surrounding area was in varying stages of construction. Eddie parked the Ford in front of the Nickols address and started up the walk. It was one of the better houses, a corner lot, and he'd almost reached the front door when he heard voices coming from the rear of the building. He took the walk skirting the corner of the house and proceeded to the patio, getting there just in time to see the Nickols children climbing into a crowded jalopy waiting at the curb. He watched them leave, and when he turned around, Mrs. Nickols was staring at him.

"Mrs. Nickols," he said, "you're looking well and the children look good."

"We're all right," she said. "We make out."

Eddie looked about. It was a very nice patio and house. The Desert Vista homes were even larger than the homes in Mountain View. Mrs. Nickols seemed to be doing well.

"I got home last night," Eddie said. "I decided to drive out and see how the new development was coming along."

But Sam Nickols' widow was no fool. She knew it wasn't an accident that he had come to this particular house.

"Mrs. Nickols," he began, "I know you probably don't like to talk about what happened; but there's something I've got to know. Did you see Sam—did you talk to him, I mean—at any time after three in the afternoon of the day he died?"

The question was unexpected. She looked puzzled.

"Three o'clock?" she echoed. "Of course. I saw Sam at dinner."

"How did he seem?"

"Seem?"

"Was he upset? Did he seem angry or worried?"

"I don't recall—" she began, and then her face brightened. "He was excited, naturally. It was the night of the election of officers at the One Hundred Sons— but I don't have to tell you that. Sam was always tense when he had to make a speech. I was so happy that his term of office was coming to an end."

"Edgy," Eddie reflected. "Yes, that would have covered it."

"Pardon, Mr. Wanamaker?"

Eddie didn't explain; instead, he asked another question.

"Then he didn't say anything to you about having had trouble with Paul that afternoon?"

"Trouble with Mr. Fenton? Why, no——"

"He didn't mention any difficulty over the Mountain View contracts?"

"I don't recall that he did. Sam and Paul Fenton had done business together for more than ten years. Why, Sam handled the plumbing contract on the first house Paul built in Emerald City—long before you came here, Mr. Wanamaker. They had troubles—certainly. Businessmen do. And then there was labor trouble——"

"I know all about that," Eddie said, "but the fact is that Sam's work ran way over the estimate on the Mountain View development—nearly $20,000 over."

"$20,000——?"

"Part of it was due to labor troubles, but Paul thought the real reason was because Sam had been taking on too many other jobs and spreading his men too far. He had it out with Sam in the office on the afternoon of the day Sam died."

Mrs. Nickols' face began to show color.

"I don't think I believe you, Mr. Wanamaker," she said.

"Nevertheless, it's the truth," Eddie insisted. "I came in while it was going on. After Sam left, Paul told me that he was canceling with Sam and intended to turn over his work to George Carlson."

"Canceling with Sam?"

"That's what Paul said. I tried to talk him out of it. I knew it would just about ruin Sam if he did, but Paul said, 'If one of us has to be ruined, it's not going to be me.'"

"Mr. Wanamaker," she broke in, "why are you telling me this?"

Eddie frowned. "Something has been troubling me for more than a year," he said. "Did Sam mention his reason for having been on Main Street just a few blocks from Paul's office on the night he was killed?"

"He'd gone for a meeting of the One Hundred Sons," she said.

"Which met in the Community Hall in Memorial Park eight blocks away."

"Sam liked to walk home—"

"Your home was on Fourth Street in the opposite direction," Eddie reminded.

"But if he'd gone to see Paul Fenton—" She paused, troubled by her own words. "No, that doesn't make sense. Mr. Fenton was at the meeting, too. Oh, I don't know! Why do you come here digging up the past, Mr. Wanamaker? I've steeled myself against holding resentment for you. Don't spoil it. If you don't care for your own sake, think of me. Whatever troubles you, please forget it."

"I'm sorry," Eddie said. "Perhaps I shouldn't have come."

"Perhaps you shouldn't—not if you think you can cause trouble between Paul Fenton and me. He's a fine man, Mr. Wanamaker. I hope you appreciate all he's done for you! I know that I appreciate what he's done for me."

Eddie had started to turn away. He stopped and looked back.

"What he's done for you?" he repeated.

"And what he's done for the children, too. What you say about Sam's work running over the estimates may be true; he had a lot of labor difficulties and lost money on those contracts himself. There wasn't much left after everything was paid off. But Mr. Fenton said that Sam's children deserved a decent home. He gave us this house, Mr. Wanamaker—clear title—just for old time's sake."

She meant him to be impressed, and he was. The house was worth at least $25,000. Paul had been generous. Beyond the patio, on the next street, a row of new houses had reached the framing stage. Eddie stared at them until he could make out the flues and the plumbing pipes.

"Mrs. Nickols," he said, "I can't make out the sign from here. Can you tell me who is doing Paul's plumbing now?"

She hesitated.

"Don't you know?"

"Yes," she said slowly, "I do know. It's George Carlson."

A name on a window and a name on a deed—two magnanimous gestures from Paul Fenton. Eddie left Sam Nickols' widow and returned to Main Street. On Sunday morning, only churchgoers and the children at the municipal pool were out. The town looked good to Eddie by daylight—his town. He drove past the Memorial Hall. Inside of it, he knew, hung a plaque on the wall displaying names of the past chairmen of the One Hundred Sons. Dr. Huston's name was there; also, Paul Fenton's, Sam Nickols', and after Sam Nickols'—

One evening, slightly over a year ago, Eddie had come home from work in a state of elation. He'd found Hilda in the kitchen, whirled her about, and given her a kiss that left her gasping for breath.

"Eddie, what is it?"

"I love you," Eddie had said.

"Yes, I know, dear, but not usually so enthusiastically. Have you been taking vitamin pills?"

And so he'd told her about his lunch with Sam Nickols', Chairman of the One Hundred Sons, and the election that was coming up in six weeks, which had suddenly become so important because Sam was putting his name in nomination for chairman. Hilda could smile and Hilda could tell him how proud she was of him; but she couldn't know what it meant to a man who had promised a town he'd stay in it and build a name for himself.

Eddie continued down Main Street. Once or twice, he caught a glimpse of a familiar face and drove past quickly. He didn't want to face his friends until he had finished what he had to do. He passed Paul's office with the significant new name on the door. Halfway down the next block, he passed Dr. Huston's office. He slowed the car to a stop and sat staring at it for some minutes.

Something seemed wrong. A large piece was missing from that fatal night; but a piece could be broken down into fragments, and fragments collected one by one.

He drove home. Dr. Huston's Cadillac was in the drive. Eddie went inside to find Hilda and her father having coffee in the kitchen. Hilda looked up, her eyes anxious.

"Eddie—where have you been?" she asked. "I was worried when I got up and found you gone. I called Dad to see if you had gone to his place. You hadn't, and so he came here."

"I drove out to the Desert Vista development to see how it was coming along," Eddie said.

"Desert Vista?"

Dr. Huston seemed interested. So did Hilda.

"Sam Nickols' widow lives out there now," Eddie added. "She has a nice house on a corner lot—Paul gave it to her, clear title."

It wasn't news to either Hilda or her father.

"Well, that's almost the truth," Dr. Huston admitted. "I suppose it seems a windfall to Mrs. Nickols, but it was actually a trade. Sam's old place, which he took in trade, isn't worth much now; but if the commercial zone creeps out that way, Paul will break even."

"Break even?" Eddie smiled crookedly. "Paul will triple his investment. That's the way Paul works. He doesn't give anything away."

"What a way to talk about Paul," Hilda scolded. "Think of all he's done for you, Eddie. He got the lawyer for your trial; he's hounded the parole board; he's done everything to help you right from the beginning."

To Hilda, the beginning was the night Sam Nickols died. Eddie's mind went back further. Six years ago, he'd felt secure enough to ask Hilda to marry him. Her answer had been Christmas with Santa Claus and all the reindeer. The next day, he told Paul. Paul said all the right words, but his face was wrong. Eddie was the intruder who had taken his girl—those were the words written on his face.

Dr. Huston's voice brought Eddie out of the past.

"Hilda's worried, Eddie. She's afraid you're going to make trouble for yourself. Drop it, man. Paul took you in as a partner to show his loyalty—and he may not make a dime out of that Fourth Street property. He merely wanted to give Sam's widow new surroundings. Paul and Sam had worked together for years. Sam put the plumbing in Paul's first house and didn't charge a cent until it was sold and paid for."

"That gave Sam a claim on Paul, didn't it?" Eddie mused.

"A claim?"

"So that if Paul had wanted to drop Sam— Maybe there was more to it than that one house. Sam might have had something on him."

"Eddie, stop it," Hilda said. "Can't you see what he's doing, Dad? He's still obsessed with the idea that he has to clear his name. Tell him to forget it, please, for the sake of—"

"Clear his name?" the doctor echoed.

"I don't remember running down Sam," Eddie said. "And there are holes in the story that came out at the trial. For instance, it was brought out that I'd taken your car, Dr. Huston, knowing, as I guess all of us know, that you keep an extra key wired to the rear bumper. But if I did take it, and that's one of the things I can't remember, where did I get it? Where was it parked?"

"At the Memorial Hall," Hilda volunteered. "It was the night of the One Hundred Sons election."

"But that's not the truth," Eddie said. "Where was it parked, Dr. Huston?"

Hilda's father hesitated. "On Main Street," he said.

"On Main Street? Why, Dr. Huston?"

"Because I was worried," Hilda broke in. "You came home early that evening. That didn't upset me—I knew you were excited about the election; but you'd been drinking, and that did upset me. You'd been drinking a lot. You had a bottle—"

"A bottle?" Eddie demanded. "A green bottle?"

"I don't know what color the bottle was. It was a

whisky bottle—a small one. You wouldn't talk to me.
You just said that it was all over."

"What was all over?"

"I don't know. I tried to get you to shower and dress
for the meeting, and that was when you went out again.
You didn't take the car; you went on foot. I thought
you would walk off whatever was bothering you and
come home, but you didn't. The meeting at the Memorial Hall started at eight. It was nearly eight-thirty when
I called Paul at the meeting—"

"Why Paul?" Eddie demanded.

"Because you work with Paul. Because I was afraid
you had been in an accident."

"I can verify that call," the doctor said. "I was in the
hall when it was made. Paul came back from the telephone and told me he had to leave for awhile. He asked
if he could use my car because the battery was dead
in his own. I gave him the keys—"

"Then it was Paul who had the car," Eddie said.

"He was looking for you," Hilda explained. "He
came back here first and then went out searching. I
wanted to go, too, but he thought it was better that
someone stay here in the event you returned. He tried
all the bars in town, and then went back to the office.
He left the car outside."

"Why didn't anyone mention this story at the trial?"
Eddie demanded.

"Because your lawyer wanted everyone to assume the
obvious: that you had come to the meeting at Memorial
Hall and then gone off in my car," Dr. Huston said.
"That concussion was your defense. If it had been
known that you were drinking before you left home that
evening, you might not have gotten off so easily."

"Is that what Paul said?"

"It's logical, isn't it?"

"Logical," Eddie mused. "Yes, in more than one
way." His face hardened, and he moved toward the
door. "Thanks," he said. "If I had known about that a
year ago—"

"Eddie," Hilda called, "where are you going?"

"To look for a bottle," Eddie said. "A green one."

Eddie went out, slamming the door behind him. Hilda started to follow, but her father objected.

"Let him go," he said. "Let him get this out of his system. He'll come back."

"But he'll start drinking again—"

Hilda broke loose and ran to the den. She dialed Paul—a surprised Paul who had imagined she and Eddie were knee-deep in some trout stream.

"Eddie insisted on coming straight home," she explained. "He's determined to learn what happened the night Sam died. He's been to see Mrs. Nickols, and he's learned from Dad that it was you who took the car."

Paul considered her words and came back brightly.

"Don't worry about it. We'll have a talk tomorrow. I've got to show a house to a client this afternoon and do some book work at the office tonight."

"No—not tonight," Hilda said.

"What's that?"

"Don't go to the office, Paul. I mean it. I'm afraid. What if Eddie remembers . . . ?"

There were seventeen bars in Emerald City, ranging from the very plush one in the new Oasis Motor Hotel to the more sedate Traveler's Bar, and on down the scale to the bare-floor variety in the Mexican section. Eddie covered them all. In the beginning he came only to question. Somewhere at some time on the night of Sam Nickols' death, he had been hit on the head with a green bottle—did any bartender recall such an incident? He couldn't expect much more than bewildered and bemused stares when he posed the question. The night was well over a year past. Most of the bartenders had forgotten Sam Nickols, few of them remembered Eddie Wanamaker—and then only by association. Paul Fenton? Did the bartender know him? At the Oasis, the response was affirmative. Paul Fenton was not only known; the night of Sam Nickols' death was remembered.

"I thought about it the next day when I read the paper," the bartender told Eddie. "Fenton came in here the night before—oh, about nine or nine-thirty. It was quiet. It's always quiet on the night when the One Hundred Sons meet—until about eleven when some of them start dropping in for a nightcap. I was surprised to see Mr. Fenton at that hour. He told me he was looking for Wanamaker."

It was dark enough at the Oasis Bar that Eddie hadn't been recognized. This wasn't a nondrinker's beat anyway.

"Had he been here?" Eddie asked.

"Not to my knowledge—that's what I told Fenton. Not to my knowledge. A good many of the local businessmen I know—Fenton, Nickols, Dr. Huston—oh, any number. But Wanamaker wasn't a drinker. That's what was brought out at the trial. Say, why all the questions? Did Wanamaker break out of prison?"

"He's trying," Eddie said.

And so Paul had gone looking for him in the most natural places to look for a man known to be out on a drunk. Somewhere they must have met, and at that place there should have been a green bottle broken. Eddie continued his inquiry as the day wore on. Afternoon turned the streets into empty corridors of heat. Only the kids in the Memorial Park pool, and a man in search of yesterday, ventured out in the midday sun. Eddie passed the Main Street office. Sometimes Paul kept it open on Sunday. He stopped at the door, but it was locked. Inside, the telephone was ringing. Without his key, Eddie could do nothing but let it ring.

It rang six times before the answering service cut in to inform Hilda that Mr. Fenton wasn't expected back until 8:00 P.M. She looked at her wristwatch. It was almost four. Her father had gone out on a call, and that meant four more hours to wait alone unless Eddie gave up and came home. And he wouldn't. She knew that.

It was nearly six o'clock before Eddie bought his first beer. He'd held out against the heat all afternoon; but at a small bar around the corner from the bus terminal, he reached the end of his hope. There was no other place to look, and no one had remembered, or wanted to admit to remembering, an incident more than a year old and of importance to only one man. He drank the beer thirstily, and it hit him like a lead fist. He hadn't eaten since breakfast, and as the warmth spread through him, a peculiar thing happened in his mind. It sharpened. It blanked out the clutter of nonessential details and came into focus. He saw a scene: a small, dark nondecorative bar. A glass in his hand and a bottle standing beside the glass. A brown bottle. Eddie ordered a second beer, pouring it carefully. Three stools away, a couple of airmen from the base were drinking beer from green bottles. Green. Eddie's mind deliberated these facts as he sipped the second beer. A green bottle had smashed against the side of his head—that was important. Paul Fenton hated him for marrying Hilda—that was important, too. To Eddie's mind, the proof of that had come when Paul wrecked his chances of becoming chairman of the One Hundred Sons.

Eddie's now very sharp mind canceled out the whole bar. Now he was in the office with Paul. It was a few minutes past three in the afternoon of the day Sam Nickols had died, and Sam had just walked out of the office.

"You can't drop Sam," Eddie had protested. "You'll ruin him if you do."

"If one of us is going to be ruined, it's not going to be me," Paul answered.

"But just because of an argument—just because you lost your head!"

"Not my head, Eddie. $20,000—that's what I've lost. I'm sorry for Sam, but he's brought this on himself. He wanted to take on extra contracts—okay, let him take them on. From now on, I'm doing business with George Carlson."

Paul was adamant. Even then, Eddie had been suspicious of his motives.

"I suppose you realize what this means to me," he said.

"To you, Eddie?" Paul asked.

"The election tonight. Sam was going to nominate me for Chairman of the One Hundred Sons. What do you suppose he's going to do now?"

To that question, Paul had given no answer at all.

Eddie looked up from his beer. The two airmen were still working on the contents of their green bottles. He felt a sudden wave of nostalgia. The uniforms changed, but the men inside the uniforms were always just as lonely. He knew the feeling well; but he'd licked it. He'd come to Emerald City and made a name for himself—only to have it taken away. And he'd learned exactly nothing for his long day's questioning. Now there was darkness outside the door. The two airmen left their stools and returned to the bus depot, and in the distance he could hear the roar of motors and the noise of people hurrying to go somewhere else. A child's voice cried out—

"Daddy, our bus is here! Daddy—"

Suddenly Eddie sat upright, tingling. There were times when something that was happening seemed to have happened before. A child crying, two green bottles on the bar—Eddie came to his feet. It had happened outside on the sidewalk. Like a man in a trance, he followed the slowly opening memory. More than a year ago, on the night of the One Hundred Sons election, he had returned to the small bar off the bus station where he'd bought those first two beers that had led him to Hilda. Perhaps the mind worked in a pattern. It hit a dead end and returned to the first haunt, just as he'd returned again tonight.

But now he was on the sidewalk. A child had cried out—but that wasn't the main thing. There had been another cry—

Look out! He's got a knife!

Now the picture came clear. It had been a sidewalk

fight between a gang of teenage toughs. He remembered
a glint of steel flashing in the light. He remembered
running forward and grabbing the wrist that held the
knife until it pointed slowly downward and finally
dropped, clattering against the sidewalk. Then he had
turned his head and caught a glimpse of the green bottle just before it smashed against his skull.

Now the memory had pain in it, a hot tongue of pain
that licked deep into the nerve fibers. Eddie's hand went
to the side of his head. Now he felt nothing but the
stubble of a quick prison haircut. He looked about,
almost dazed. He was on the sidewalk outside the terminal bar—yes; but there were no young hoodlums
racing off into the darkness now, and no broken glass
on the sidewalk. It was a year later, and he knew how
he'd gotten his concussion on the night Sam Nickols
died. But what had happened next? He was still blocks
away from the place where Paul had parked Dr. Huston's car. Like a man in a trance, Eddie walked back
to here he had left the Ford.

At eight o'clock, Hilda telephoned Paul's office again.
This time, Paul answered. No, he hadn't seen Eddie.
No, he hadn't heard from Eddie. Yes, he had talked to
Mrs. Nickols. No, he couldn't leave the office just yet.
He had an important letter to write. What could Eddie
do if he did come to the office? They would have a talk,
and Paul would send him home.

"But if he's been drinking," Hilda protested. "You
know how he gets on just one or two beers."

"Let me worry about that," Paul assured her. "I have
a couple of letters to finish and then I'll leave. I'll drop
by on my way home and help you look for Eddie. He
can't have gone far."

Hilda replaced the telephone in the cradle and sat
for a few seconds in a silence that became more terrible the longer it lasted. When she could endure it no
longer, she took a wrap from the hall closet and went
out into the darkness. She walked rapidly toward Main
Street. . . .

Paul Fenton. It was peculiar how Eddie could think only one name, and how he could feel only the blow on his head that had landed over a year ago. It was as if time had spun backward, and this was the night of the banquet of the One Hundred Sons. Paul Fenton. The name was like a magnet, and the power of the magnet was hatred. Why did he hate Paul so much? Because of the year in jail? No, time had spun backwards. It was the night of the One Hundred Sons dinner, and he hadn't attended because Paul Fenton had evened the score of losing Hilda by denying Eddie the one honor that would make them equals. That was what gave the magnet its power.

Paul Fenton. Eddie drove to Main Street and turned left. Now he was acting out a part that had been played before. It wasn't as late as it had been a year ago; but it was Sunday, and that meant the streets were just as dark and just as empty. Eddie drove slowly until he saw the light in Paul's office. He pulled to the curb and waited, his fingers gripping the steering wheel. He wasn't sure what he wanted to do until the light vanished and Paul stepped out of the office. Paul hesitated long enough to lock the door, then turned and began to walk toward the street light. He carried something in his hands—letters. He would have to cross the street at the end of the block to mail them, and it was late and the streets empty.

Eddie had kept the motor running, but the lights were switched off. He left them off and eased the Ford away from the curb. Paul had reached the corner. He paused before starting to cross the street, but he didn't notice a vehicle without lights. Eddie had only to gun the motor . . .

"Eddie—don't! Paul—look out!"

Eddie heard Hilda's cry even before he saw her; and when he saw her, he could do nothing but hit the brakes and thank God when the Ford stopped in time. She had come out of the shadows, crying her warning and running directly in front of the car; but it wasn't the sight or the sound of her that put an end to Eddie's

search for fragments—it was the truth. He sat back,
trembling before the sudden realization of what he'd
done one year ago. . . .

Paul unlocked the office, and Hilda helped Eddie to
a chair. He wasn't hurt and he wasn't drunk any more,
but he was more afraid than he had ever been in his life.
Eddie was no coward. An enemy outside was nothing
to fear, but an enemy within— He looked up at Hilda's
face.

"You knew the truth, didn't you?" he said.

"I tried to tell you to forget," she answered.

"But you knew that I had murdered Sam Nickols."

"No, Eddie. Not murder."

"Yes, murder," Eddie insisted. "I remembered the
whole thing a few minutes ago. I came down Main
Street. It was dark and empty, and then I saw someone
come out of the office, just as I did tonight. I thought
it was Paul. I wanted to kill him."

"Eddie—"

"I wanted to kill him," Eddie repeated. "And then
I saw your father's car parked at the curb and remembered where he kept the extra key. I ran Sam down de-
liberately—not accidentally. I want to kill Paul—"

Eddie turned his head and looked at Paul. Like
Hilda, Paul had known the truth, too. He must have
seen the accident from the office and kept the secret of
the truth all this time. Why? For forgiveness? Or because he had hated Eddie Wanamaker and knew that
his hate had helped kill Sam Nickols? Behind Paul
the new name on the window told a grim joke. Partners. Yes, they were partners all right.

There was only one more thing that Eddie needed
to know.

"Why did Sam come here the night he was killed?"
he asked.

"For the same reason I came," Paul said. "Looking
for you."

"For me? Why?"

Not for the reason Paul had come looking for him—

not because Hilda had asked it. There could be only one reason for Sam's having come, and Eddie sensed it before Paul could answer.

"Sam didn't hold my decision to drop his contract against you, Eddie," he said. "After I left the meeting, he put your name in nomination. He just dropped by to leave word that you had been elected chairman of the One Hundred Sons."

THE VAPOR CLUE

by James Holding, Jr.

If you want to go to Washingtonville, Pennsylvania, you go east from Pittsburgh on Route 78 for about twenty miles toward the Riverton entrance to the Pennsylvania Turnpike. As you approach Washingtonville, you dip down past a big new shopping center and run along the bottom of a shallow valley past seven gas stations, three roadside markets, two branch banks, a yard full of trailer rigs waiting for assignment, and several fairly clean cafes that cater largely to truck drivers.

Just before you lift out of this shallow valley over the western ridge, you can quickly look to your left and see the huddle of houses just off the highway that is Washingtonville itself. And because the accident happened on Highway 78 within shouting distance, almost, of Washingtonville City Hall, it was the Washingtonville Police who had jurisdiction and Lieutenant Randall who was largely responsible for handling the case. Randall would never have caught up with the killer without the help of a waitress named Sarah Benson.

At 5:30 A.M. on December 16th, a 1954 Plymouth sedan, following Route 78 east, labored heavily up the slope of the ridge that formed the western boundary of Washingtonville's little valley. The car had engine trouble; the motor was running very unevenly and the car jerked and hesitated in its progress. The road had been plowed clean of yesterday's five-inch snowfall, but piles of snow edged the highway and the still-dark morning was bitter cold.

Inside the sedan, Hub Grant said to his wife, "If I can coax her up this hill and over, maybe we can find a gas station or garage open on the other side. We've sure got to get something done to this baby before we can make Connecticut in it."

His wife nodded anxiously. "It's so early, Hub. I'm afraid nothing will be open yet. We should have stopped at one of those motels back there."

"I wish we had," Hub admitted.

The car topped the ridge. Washingtonville's valley lay before them, snow-covered, silent, and marked by only a few lonesome-looking lights along the highway ahead.

Hub said, "There's a gas station. Let's try it."

He urged the reluctant car toward Amos White's gas station halfway down the gentle slope of the hill. And the Plymouth's engine chose that moment to conk out completely.

Hub took advantage of his downhill momentum to pull to the edge of the highway, where the car buried its right wheels in a bank of plow-piled snow and came to a cushioned stop. Hub opened his door and got out into the chilly darkness. No sign of dawn showed yet. He walked into Amos White's service station and saw that it was deserted. Amos didn't open up until seven o'clock these winter mornings.

Hub came back to the car. "Nobody there." He looked down the road toward Washingtonville's sparse lights. "Guess I'll try down in the valley. Looks like something might be open." He beat his arms against his sides. "Boy, it's cold out here! You sit there and wait for me, honey, and keep the doors locked. Okay?"

"Okay," she said. "I'll wait here."

"I won't be long, I hope." He slammed the car door and walked down the road toward the shopping center.

It was 5:41.

At that moment, Sarah Benson was walking from her home on Washingtonville's outskirts toward the concrete ribbon of Highway 78 where it touched the periphery of the town at the shopping center. Sarah was bundled up in a heavy plaid coat and wore a green scarf over her titian hair. It was her week to open up Wright's Truckers' Rest and prepare the first enormous urn of coffee for the sleepy, chilled truck drivers who would soon begin arriving. They were regular customers, most of them; they knew that Wright's opened at 6:00 A.M. sharp, that Wright's coffee was good and hot, and that Sarah Benson was the best-looking waitress between New York and Chicago.

When she reached the highway, Sarah walked toward Wright's cafe, a hundred yards down the road from the shopping-center parking lot. It was awfully cold, must be near zero, she thought. And still dark. No one was about. Only an occasional car or truck swished past her on the concrete. She was reaching into her bag for the key to Wright's cafe when she heard a man's footsteps on the road behind her.

She turned in surprise and saw a dark form approaching from the west, his lanky figure silhouetted for her against the snow bank that edged the highway. He saw her at the same time, apparently. For he lifted an arm and called, "Hey, there . . . !"

Whatever he intended to say, he never finished it. A car rocketed down the highway toward him, coming fast on the outside right-hand lane of Route 78, the one he was walking in. He was suddenly caught in the beam of the approaching car's headlights. Sarah could see him make a startled move toward the snow bank beside him to avoid the onrushing vehicle. But he was too late.

Transfixed by horror, Sarah watched the car swerve wildly as the driver applied his brakes with a scream of rubber against the road; she saw in slow-motion detail the heavy, pinwheeling arc described by the pedestrian's body after the sickening sound of its impact against the car's bumper; she saw the body come to rest in grotesque, spread-eagled limpness on the snow bank not twenty yards from where she stood.

It was only as a dazed after-thought that she looked at the car again. It slowed almost to a halt, its stop-lights glowing red, and Sarah thought it would stop. But then, with a snarl of desperately applied power, it gathered speed and made off down the highway toward the eastern ridge of the valley.

Sarah couldn't believe her eyes. "Stop!" she shrieked after the vanishing car. "Stop!" She thought she was going to be ill. "You hit a man!" Even while she screamed, the taillights of the murder car winked out over the eastern ridge.

Sarah tried to control the trembling of her legs and the heaving of her stomach. She ran to the motionless man in the snow bank. When she saw that nothing could be done for him, she returned to the cafe, opened the door with her key, switched on the lights inside, and telephoned the Washingtonville police.

It was 5:55.

Lieutenant Randall and the police ambulance arrived at the scene of the accident at 6:05, just as the first faint glimmer of daylight showed. By then, a lot of cars and a truck had stopped beside the snow bank, drawn by the sight of the spread-eagled body and the bloodied snow, and by Sarah Benson's slim figure standing beside it, waiting for the law.

When Randall arrived, he detailed a policeman to send the curious on their way when it was certain none of them had witnessed the accident, and dispatched the hit-run victim to Washingtonville Hospital, where he was pronounced dead on arrival of multiple external and internal injuries, including a smashed skull.

Randall sat down at the counter of Wright's Truckers' Rest and talked earnestly with the only witness to the accident, Miss Sarah Benson. She was being as helpful as she could, though she was still pale from shock and wisely sipping a cup of her own coffee, black, to settle her nerves.

Randall was full of driving urge to get a description of the murder car as quickly as possible, but even so, he couldn't help noticing with approval how pretty Sarah Benson was—how well her titian hair set off her creamy skin and level blue eyes.

"What kind of a car was it?" he asked her.

"I don't know. It was dark. And coming toward me, the headlights blinded me. I couldn't tell anything about it."

He sighed. "I was afraid of that. But after you saw the car hit the man, you looked at the car again, you say . . . as it was going away from you?"

"Yes, I did."

"And you didn't recognize its make?"

"No. It seemed to be a dark-colored sedan, all one tone. That's all I can be sure of. And that its stoplights were on, bright red, before the driver decided to run away."

"Those stoplights," Randall said. "What shape were they?"

"Round, I guess," Sarah said.

"You guess? Don't you know?"

"No, I can't be sure."

"Big and round, or small and round?" Randall insisted.

"Medium and round, I guess," said Sarah. "I didn't really notice. I was so shocked . . ."

"You saw the back of the car," Randall interrupted her rudely, "with the stoplights on and nothing between you and the car. Surely you saw the license number or at least the license plate. Think hard, please."

"I'm thinking, Lieutenant."

"Well, was it a Pennsylvania license? Or New York?" He was still hopeful. "Did you see it?"

She shook her head slowly. "I'm afraid not."

"Damn it," Randall said, "you *must* have!"

She smiled at him sympathetically, conscious of how anxious he was to elicit a description of the car from her. "No," she said very quietly, "I didn't see any license plate."

He flushed. "I'm sorry, Miss Benson. But a description of the car, *some* description, is essential if we're to have any chance at all of catching this man. You understand that, don't you? If you didn't see the license plate, did you notice anything else about the car? A dent in the rear fender, maybe, a cracked back window, luminous tape on the bumper, anything at all?"

She closed her eyes and conjured up the horror of fifteen minutes ago. She was silent for a long time. Then she opened her eyes and said, "I can't remember anything more. There was this cloud of white steam coming out of the car's exhaust pipe and it sort of hid the back of the car, I guess."

Randall stood up. "Well, thanks very much. We'll have to do the best we can with a general description. There is evidence of damage to the front end of the car. We found a piece of metal in the road that broke off the grill." He turned to go, then paused. "Could you come down to headquarters sometime today and sign a statement? It will be helpful to have an official eyewitness record."

Sarah finished the last of her coffee and reached for her coat on a hook behind the counter. "I'll come now," she said. "Jenny can handle things here until I get back." Jenny was a sallow-complexioned bottle blonde already serving coffee and doughnuts to four drivers at the far end of Wright's long counter.

"Good," said Randall, "I'll drive you in. Come along."

It was 6:24.

When Amos White arrived at 6:45 to open up his gas station for the day, he found a Plymouth sedan stuck in the snow right beside the apron to his place with a young woman sitting alone in the front seat, her chin in her upturned coat collar for warmth and a very worried look in her eyes.

Amos unlocked his service room. The young lady climbed out of the car and came in and asked in a timid voice if she could use his telephone. Amos said

yes, and heard her call the police. And he kindly helped
her over the first awful moments when she discovered
from the police that she was a widow . . . that Hub
Grant, her husband, had been killed by a hit-run driver,
identity so far unknown.

Amos' watch said seven o'clock.

All these events occurred in a little more than an
hour in Washingtonville on the morning of December
16th. Then, for the subsequent six hours until one
o'clock, nothing happened at all.

At least, it seemed that way to Lieutenant Randall.
Of course, he flashed his meager description of the
wanted car to state, county and turnpike police and
asked their cooperation in spotting and holding the car
and driver. And he fine-tooth-combed the stretch of
Highway 78 between the shopping center and the eastern ridge in the forlorn hope of locating another witness
who could come up with a better description of the hit-
run car than Sarah Benson had been able to supply.

But he had no luck.

That is, he had no luck until one o'clock, at which
time he was eating a ham-on-rye at his desk at headquarters waiting for some word on the car. The desk
sergeant downstairs called him and said there was a
woman to see him. When she came into his office, it
was Sarah Benson.

He hastily swallowed the bite of sandwich he was
working on and stood up awkwardly. "Well," he said.
"You again, Sarah."

She raised smooth brows at his use of her first name
but didn't comment on it. She sat in a straight chair
across from his desk. "Me again, Lieutenant. I've
thought of something that may prove helpful."

"Good for you," he said. "What is it?"

"You remember my statement about the car . . ." she
began tentatively.

"Sure." He took the typed statement off his desk and
handed it to her. "What about it?"

She read slowly from the statement: "A cloud of

white steam was coming out of the car's exhaust and I couldn't see the license plate or any other identifying marks."

Randall stared at her. "So what? You told me that this morning. The car smoked. Probably needs a ring job. I've already given the boys that information."

A lively animation marked her manner now. "That cloud of steam," she said, leaning forward in her chair, "wasn't an oily kind of smoke. It was whiter, like mist, as I told you. Or the white vapor that your breath makes on a cold morning."

Randall said, "Yes? And what about this white vapor?"

She replied indirectly. "You know Wright's, where I work? It's right across the highway from Jensen's trucking depot, where all his trucks stand waiting for loads."

He nodded.

"Well, I've watched those trucks go out on cold days. And it occurred to me that after they've sat in the yard all night in the cold, their exhaust smoke looks just like what the hit-run car was giving out this morning."

Randall merely stared at her in puzzlement.

"And when trucks drive into our place after running all night, they never give out that white exhaust vapor."

Randall's eyes widened and he sat bolt upright in his chair. "Hey!" he exclaimed.

She smiled at him. "That's right," she said. "I called my brother on the phone to check it. He's a mechanic in a garage in Pittsburgh. And he says that's right."

Randall swung around in his chair, grabbing for his phone. Over his shoulder he said, dismissing her, "Thanks a million, Sarah. I'll call you."

When he called her later, at her home, she answered herself. "Oh, hello, Lieutenant Randall," she greeted him. "Any news?"

"Plenty," he said with satisfaction. "The state police picked him up outside of Allentown an hour ago, thanks to you, Sarah. His car has a dented front end, a broken grill that ought to match up with the piece of metal we found in the road, and traces of blood and hair. We've got the whole thing lined out." He hesitated in unaccustomed embarrassment. "I'd like to tell you about it, Sarah."

"Go ahead, Lieutenant," she answered. "I'm listening."

"Well, I mean . . ." He rubbed a hand over his hair irritably. "Personally."

She ignored that. "Then the clue of the white vapor *did* help?" He thought he detected a teasing note.

"Sure it helped." His own voice was laced with chagrin. "Until you called it to my attention, it never occurred to me that white steam from an exhaust pipe in cold weather usually means that the car motor has only very recently been started. I kept thinking of the hit-run car as one from a distance, passing through here without stopping. But the white exhaust vapor made it clear that the guilty driver was either a local, or somebody who had stayed here all night. Because it showed that his car engine had just been started before the accident . . . and had been sitting in the cold for some time quite close to the accident scene, I tried the simplest thing first, and hit pay dirt right away."

"Where *did* the car start from?" she asked.

"The Buena Vista Motel. The fellow pulled in there at three yesterday afternoon from the west, slept till five this morning and started out again. His was the only car that left any of our local motels or hotels that early this morning. He was driving a dark blue Ford sedan, Pennsylvania license number VN 167. It was all on the record at the Buena Vista. After I fed that information to the boys, they had him in twenty minutes."

"Good," she said.

He changed the subject abruptly. "Why did you go to all that trouble—to telephone your brother and so on—just to be helpful to the police?"

"Because I wanted to help you catch that hit-run driver." Remembered horror was in her voice. Then she laughed a little. "And besides," she added, "I took a liking to you, Lieutenant."

"Good," said Randall. "Fine. I hoped that might be part of it. I've got another idea I'd like to check with you now."

"If it's the same idea that my truck drivers get about me, you can forget it," she said.

He cleared his throat. "I think you have a flair for police work, Sarah. Can't I take you to dinner tonight so we can talk it over?"

She hesitated only long enough to worry him slightly. Then she said softly, "That would be lovely."

Randall cradled his phone and glanced at the round, discolored police clock on his office wall. It said 5:45.

WETBACK

by Murray Wolf

I will tell it now. All of it, and I hope well enough. It has taken five years to learn to tell it. Five years from the time of the knife to this time of the pen. . . .

It was summer and Antonio laughed at me. It was the night of the party that my cousin Antonio laughed at me because I wouldn't come away from the window, because I kept staring out over the city, at the buildings and the lights that went on and on into the distance, until the haze swallowed them up.

"Come away from the window, Juan," Antonio said. "The city won't go away."

His friends laughed with him.

"Maybe he's afraid he'll go away," Pepe said. "Maybe he's afraid the border police will catch him, send him back to Mexico."

I turned away from the city toward them, for a moment feeling a cold ache in my stomach. Yes, I thought, that's what I'm afraid of, even if Antonio says it's silly. Antonio says I'm here now, all I've got to do is learn English and I'll be all right.

"Squares I've seen before," Miguel said. "But this one . . ."

"This one is my cousin," Antonio said. His voice wasn't laughing now. He leaned toward Miguel, a strange, almost angry look on his face.

"Sure," Miguel said. "Sure."

They lapsed back into English. I tried to listen, to understand them, but I couldn't understand too much. They were drinking wine, the same red wine I'd drunk at home, in San Ysidro, in the mountains of Sonora; the room had many of the home smells, wine and chili and garlic. But it wasn't like my village.

I stared out over Los Angeles, toward the palm trees and the endless traffic and the people, so many people, more than I had ever imagined living in the entire world.

My cousin Antonio didn't know how lucky he was. He was just my age, seventeen, three months younger than I, actually; yet already he had a big room of his own, with space for a cot and a chair and a table, a room he could visit his friends in without Mama and Papa and his sisters underfoot. He had good clothes, too. He and his friends all had shiny purple jackets, with bulls' heads on them. *"Baje Los Toros,"* the jackets said. "Down with the Bulls." Antonio said it was a joke.

"Come, Juan," Antonio called. "Have some wine."

I shook my head. "Later."

"He's drunk with the bright lights," Miguel said. Pepe laughed with him. My cousin didn't laugh, and after a minute the other two stopped and they were all quiet.

Two weeks I've been here, I thought, fifteen days since I crossed the border. . . . The village seemed far, far away in time. It was hard to believe that there, at home, my mother and my little brothers would be eating dinner as usual and maybe wondering where I was. . . . I'll never go back, I promised myself, staring out past the fire escape, over the roof of the house in front, across Chavez Ravine to the high buildings and the endless streams of cars on the freeway below. Maybe later, I thought, when I have the money, I can send for Mama and the boys.

I was just thinking this, looking forward to the day when I could mail the money home, when I heard the knock on the door. It was the knock all of Antonio's friends used, two quick raps, a pause, and then two more.

"Come in," Antonio called.

The door opened and Antonio's other friend, the short, chunky one they called Switch, stepped inside. I was sorry, in a way, that he was there. I didn't like Switch, though I'd never mentioned how I felt to Antonio. Why should I speak against my cousin's friends? But Switch had a loose mouth; he called girls *putas*, and not only the girls from Mama Ortegas'. I'd heard him speak of Antonio's sister Rosa this way once, and Rosa was a good girl, like an iceberg when you told her nice things. Once I'd seen him try to pinch Rosa; she'd hit him and said, "I'll tell my brother," and Switch had just laughed and walked away.

"That all you can do?" Switch said. "Sit around and swill wine, like old men?"

"What else?" my cousin said. "We should go to the YMCA, maybe?"

They all laughed. I laughed, too, to be polite, though I didn't understand the joke. Switch dropped down on the cot beside my cousin and reached for the wine bottle.

"I know of a party," he said. "They've got lots of food, lots of liquor—they can't ever put it all away without help."

"Who?" Antonio said. "Some of the Aces?"

"It's too hot for a rumble," Miguel said, reaching for the wine.

"No," Switch said. "Not the Aces. It's a private party. One of the anglo kids is giving it. You know, Terry Fletcher, over on Avenue 60."

"Might be an idea," Pepe said. "They'd be real glad to see us, wouldn't they?"

"Yeah," Switch said. "Real glad."

Miguel reached for his purple jacket. He'd taken it off earlier, when he'd said it was too hot.

"What're we waiting for?" he asked.

My cousin hesitated. He looked over at me, then at the others.

"I don't know about Juan," he said uncertainly.

"Oh, bring the kid along." Switch turned to me. "You'd like to go to an honest-to-God American birthday party, wouldn't you, kid?"

I didn't like the way he said it, the half-smile on his face, but then, I never liked the way Switch said anything.

"Is it a fiesta?" I said.

"Yeah. That's just what it's going to be. A fiesta."

"I'd like to go," I said.

Antonio hesitated. Then he turned and went over to his closet and pulled out a purple jacket. One of the sleeves was torn and the colors were faded, but it had the bull's head on the back.

"Good I didn't throw this away," Antonio said. "Here, Juan. Put this on."

It was a little tight over my shoulders, but I didn't care. I zipped it up and turned back and forth, looking at my reflection in the cracked glass hanging on the closet door. Now I look like an Americano, I thought. For the first time.

"Come on," Switch said.

In the room outside, the family room where Mama Lopez had just finished cleaning up after dinner, Rosa stood watching us.

"Hi, baby," Switch said in English.

She turned away from him. Her glance slid past Pepe and Miguel and her brother; it started to slide past me but stopped.

"Juan, you going with them?" she asked, and stared at me.

I wondered why her voice sounded so sad.

"Yes," I said. "We're going to a party."

For the first time, she reached out to me. Her hand was soft against mine. She was so pretty it hurt to look at her, just at the stage where a girl starts turning into a woman. She smelled of soap and perfume and, underneath, the soft woman-smell the girls of San Ysidro had.

"Don't go, Juan."

Switch laughed.

Mama Lopez swung around toward him, as if about to say something, then tossed her head angrily and turned away.

"You want to go to the party, Rosa?" I said.

"No." She pulled her hand away and turned her back on me.

"Come on." Antonio started for the door. He sounded embarrassed.

I followed them, out into the street. I wished Rosa could have come with us, but maybe it wasn't the custom for girls to go to this kind of party. I couldn't get used to the customs, here in Los Angeles.

By now, after two weeks, I was no longer so terrified of the cars, the way my cousin drove, cutting in and out of traffic on the freeway, with other drivers honking and yelling at him. Besides, just about the time I really began to get scared, we pulled off the freeway and turned up a wide, quiet street, with big houses on either side, and lawns and rows of flowers and trees.

At the end of the block, one house was all lit up. Music poured out the open windows, the strange gringo music I'd never really learned to like. I heard laughter, both men's and women's, and I wondered, as we pulled up to park in front, why we couldn't have brought Rosa. Unless maybe the women here were from Mama Ortegas'. . . .

"That's Luis' car up ahead," Switch said. "I told him and the Barros to meet us here. Better to have seven, eight guys, play it cool. . . ."

We walked toward the house, toward the music and the laughter. From the other car three boys whom I'd never seen before got out and fell in beside us. They wore the purple jackets, too.

"Do we knock?" one of them said.

"No," Switch said. "We walk right in."

I straightened my shoulders in the tight jacket as he pushed the door open. Inside, all I could see at first was a very big room, like something out of the moving pictures, with the furniture pushed back and couples dancing. There were so many girls in bright dresses it was hard to look on any one of them.

The others pushed past me inside. I just stood in the doorway, staring. I'd never dreamed the party would be like this. I'd never dreamed a house would be like this, except maybe in Hollywood—all shiny floors and great windows that filled up a whole wall and, beyond one window, a floodlighted terrace with a swimming pool.

I don't know how long I stared before the music stopped and first one, then another, of the dancers swung around and faced us. The room had been full of noise, people talking and laughing over the music. As they turned to us, the laughter stopped.

"What's the matter?" I said, in Spanish. No one answered me.

Switch was walking across the room, toward the table loaded with food that stood at the far end, up against a wall that was solid wood instead of a window. As he went toward it, the people fell back away from him, opening up an aisle for him to walk through, toward the table.

At the far end of the room, a boy stood waiting. There was a girl with him, but she stepped behind him as Switch came up, so that all I could see was the boy.

"Hello, Terry," Switch said.

"What are you doing here?" I understood enough English to know what he was saying, but I didn't understand why his voice was so choked up.

"Oh, we knew it was just a mistake you didn't send us invitations, Terry. We knew you'd want us to come. . . ."

It was so quiet I could hear the people out on the terrace splashing in the pool. Somebody dived off the high board and hit wrong, the water flying up all over, and a couple of girls in bright bathing caps laughed. They didn't even glance toward the house. They hadn't seen us yet.

"Okay, Switch," Terry said. "Okay."

He stepped back away from the table and waved his hands at the food, lots of bits of meat sliced up real small and little fishes and cheese and other things I didn't recognize.

"Help yourselves."

My cousin Antonio picked up some bread and a slice of meat.

"That's just what we're going to do," he said. His voice didn't sound at all like it usually did; it was rough like coarse sand.

He's scared, too, I thought. It made me feel better, to realize that my cousin, who'd been born in Los Angeles, was nervous in a house like this one. I smiled and went over to the nearest couple.

"Hello," I said. "I'm Juan." It still seemed strange, hearing my own voice say things in English.

The girl backed away from me. The boy with her, a blond kid about my age, muttered, "Hello," and then sort of looked past me, as if I wasn't there. His Adam's apple kept jumping up and down in his throat.

Up where Switch was, an older man and woman had just come in from some room in the back. The man put his hand on Terry Fletcher's shoulder.

"I'm Ralph Fletcher," he said. His voice sounded very loud over the quiet in the room. "This is my house. I don't think I, or my son, invited you into it."

"Oh, don't feel bad, Mr. Fletcher," Switch said. "We don't carry grudges."

The woman kept edging sideways, toward the telephone on the stand by the table. Switch stepped between her and it. He was smiling, more happy-looking than I'd ever seen him, as he reached into his pocket and pulled out his knife.

The woman froze. She let out a little gasp and stepped back, toward the man.

"Easy, Martha," Mr. Fletcher said.

Switch snapped the blade open. If anything, the room grew stiller than ever. He made me nervous, too, and I'd seen him play with the knife before; he was always playing with it, sometimes throwing it, but more often just snapping it open and shut.

"You wouldn't want to call anyone, now would you,

Mrs. Fletcher?" he asked. "You wouldn't want to bi
up the party? . . ."

He picked up the telephone cord and held it in his
left hand.

"Course you wouldn't," he said, snapping the knife
down into the cord. The two cut halves fell loose at his
feet. Why should he cut the cord? This I did not understand—not at all.

"Start up the music!" he cried. "Let's have some
fun!"

My cousin Antonio grabbed hold of the girl beside
him. The boy she was with started to protest, then
backed off. The music started up, a *baile* this time,
with the good strong beat I'd always liked to hear,
fiesta music. The girl was pretty stiff, but Antonio was
a wonderful dancer. He knew all the steps. He led her
through them, while the kids at the party stood back
and watched them. Anyone, I thought, would stop to
watch my cousin, when he was really dancing.

After a while Pepe and Miguel and the others joined
in. Switch just stood by the table, talking to Mr. and
Mrs. Fletcher; I couldn't hear what he was saying, over
the music. Then he swung around, facing out at the
kids who'd been at the party before us.

"Hey, you squares, you dance, too. Don't just stand
there gawking. . . ."

The party started up again, with everyone dancing,
but somehow it wasn't the same as before. For one
thing, no one was laughing. I thought it must be because
of Switch and his knife.

I turned to the girl I'd said hello to earlier. She looked
frightened.

"You want to dance?" I said.

She didn't answer. The boy she was with pushed her
forward.

"Don't make them mad," he said.

I danced with her until the music changed, but it
wasn't much fun. She was like lead in my arms. I
thought, no, this girl isn't from Mama Ortegas' or anywhere like that; she's too unfriendly. I tried dancing

with another girl, but it wasn't any better. If only I'd brought Rosa, I thought. She'd probably never been to a party like this.

After awhile I grew tired of dancing. Somehow, the longer I stayed at the party, the more disappointing it became. It didn't seem like a fiesta. No one was having fun. I kept thinking, they were having fun until we came. Maybe we should have stayed away. Maybe they didn't want us.

It made me feel bad, thinking like that. Even my purple jacket didn't help. I went outside, past Mrs. Fletcher, who looked very white and sort of sick, out onto the terrace. Something was wrong, this I knew for a certainty. What—I didn't know.

No one was swimming now. The kids had all come out of the pool and were huddled back at the far end of the terrace, by the diving boards. Then I saw Switch. He was down at the far end of the pool, beside a little house that first I thought must be for the plumbing and then I realized probably wasn't, not here. He was talking to a girl.

My cousin Antonio was dancing and I didn't want to bother him. Pepe and Miguel were dancing too. I thought, I want to go home. I don't like the party; it doesn't have the fiesta mood, at least, not for me. I don't belong here.

I wanted to tell someone I was leaving. I didn't want my cousin to worry about me later. I started over toward Switch. Though I did not like to speak to him, he was near.

As I moved to him, he pushed open the door of the little house and stepped in, pulling the girl after him. She started to cry out; then I heard her voice choke off as if Switch's hand had come over her mouth. I stopped and looked back, toward the boys at the other end of the pool. They were too far away; they hadn't heard anything. Probably, they hadn't seen anything either.

I didn't know what to do. Maybe this sort of thing always happened at parties in Los Angeles. I doubted it, though. My cousin Antonio wouldn't make a girl go with him, I thought, not if she was crying. I remembered the day Switch had pinched Rosa, and how mad she'd been.

"Hey!" I called. "Switch!"

The door to the little house was unlocked. I pulled it open and went in after him. Inside it was very dark; all I could see was the vague outline of furniture and, against the far wall, two figures struggling. I could hear the girl's muffled cries.

"You let her go," I said.

"Keep out of this, kid. . . ."

I could see them now, Switch holding the girl's hands pinned behind her with one of his hands, while the other was over her mouth.

"You get out," he said.

"Not till you let her go."

"Why are you worried over her? She's just a *puta.*"

"Then why's she crying?"

I started toward him. There wasn't any use arguing with him, I knew. I'd have to make him let her go. I knew now that I'd been right when I'd disliked Switch, when I'd wondered why he was my cousin's friend. He was bad.

He had been holding the girl tight against him, much too tight. As I came up, he pushed her roughly away. He reached into his pocket and I saw, in the dim light, the knife flash out.

"I told you to get out, kid. . . ."

The girl huddled back against the wall. Her dress was ripped down from the shoulder, clear across her breast; for a moment, she didn't seem to realize it. I saw her slight figure and thought, she's no *puta,* she's a child—and just then she sobbed and covered her breast with her hands and shrank back still farther away from us.

I kept coming, toward the knife. I didn't feel mixed up now. I didn't feel I had to make excuses for Switch. He was bad; there couldn't be any doubts now that he was bad. I had to help the girl.

The knife blade flashed out at me. I laughed. I'd

played with knives myself, in the mountains.

I jumped to the side and the knife went by me. I'd misjudged though; I felt it rip through the elbow of my purple jacket. Then, before Switch could hit again, I grabbed his wrist with one hand and his upper arm with the other and levered him forward at the same time I kicked him.

He screamed as he fell. I didn't know if I'd broken his arm or not. I didn't care.

"You fight with knives," I said, "you should learn to use them better."

There were a dozen men around my village better than Switch. Even I was better, and I didn't like knives.

He kept moaning, on the floor. I picked up his knife and snapped the blade shut and put it in my jacket pocket. Then I reached out to the girl.

She backed away from me. She kept on crying, her hands over her breast. She was still crying when I carried Switch outside and dumped him down in the bright lights of the terrace.

The Fletchers were the first to come over to me. They stood staring down at Switch. After a minute, the couples started coming over, leaving the dance floor and crowding out around the pool.

"I'm sorry," I said. "He tried to hurt the girl."

She had followed me outside. She held up her torn dress and stared down at Switch. She had stopped crying, finally, and I was glad. I hated to see girls cry.

My cousin Antonio was staring at me across the crowd. He had a very strange look on his face, almost as if he hated me.

"We'd better leave," I said to him, in Spanish. "I don't think they'll want any of us here now."

Antonio disappeared in the crowd. I looked around. I didn't see any purple jackets anywhere, except Switch. I wondered if I should leave by myself and try to find my way back to my cousin's or whether I should stay with Switch.

While I was still thinking about it, I heard the sirens. The police were inside the house, coming toward me, before I realized what the sirens meant. I felt, all of a sudden, terribly frightened. They've come to take me back, I thought; they'll send me back to the village. I turned to run, but the wall reached clear around the terrace and there was no way out except past the uniformed men who were coming toward me.

I stared around me, at the beautiful house and the girls in their rich, soft clothes, and I thought, If they send me back I'll never see this again. Never.

"Don't be afraid," Mr. Fletcher said. "I'll tell them what you did. I'll tell them you helped us."

I didn't understand. I just stood there, with all the anglo kids staring at me and talking in English much too fast for me to understand them. Then the policemen had closed in around me and one of them grabbed hold of my arm.

"Okay, come on, you."

The boys and girls stood back away from us as they led me out. Behind me, I could hear Switch crying and cursing as they dragged him after me. I felt ashamed.

"I'm sorry," I said. "I'm sorry we ruined your party."

They didn't answer me.

In the police car, going down to the jail, Switch turned his back on me. I was just as glad. I had enough troubles. The handcuffs made me feel I'd done something really bad, for which I'd be punished. Something much worse than just slipping across the border without papers. The police car turned onto the freeway, and the city began sliding past us, and, finally, the lights of the police building were just ahead.

I wanted to jump from the car, run out into the city and keep on running. But I couldn't. I knew there was nothing I could do now.

Once we reached the jail, two of the policemen took me away from Switch, into a little room. They started asking me questions about what had happened, but they were talking English much too fast and I couldn't quite understand. I shook my head.

"Get Jose," one of them said. "He can talk to the kid."

I didn't know what I should do. I didn't know if I should tell them about Switch or not. After all, he was my cousin's friend. Then I saw the door open and the Fletchers come in, the father and the mother and the son. I looked down, at my hands.

Mr. Fletcher came over to me.

"I wanted to thank you," he said. "I wanted to tell you I'd help you, if I can."

"Is the girl all right?" I said.

"She's pretty upset," he said. "You know what could have happened."

I nodded. I thought of Rosa, backing away from Switch. I thought of how Rosa always avoided him, of how she'd never stay around if he was in the house, unless Antonio was there.

"He's bad," I said.

A policeman who had just come into the room walked over to me. He was Mexican; it made me feel better to see him.

"Yes," he said in Spanish. "He's bad, all right." And then he asked me what had happened.

I found myself telling the Mexican policeman everything. He wasn't rough, like the others; he didn't yell at me. He just kept nodding his head and saying, "Yes, I see why you did that. Yes, I understand. . . ."

I felt better when I'd told him. I felt better still when they put me in a cell all by myself, where I didn't have to listen to Switch cursing at me.

In the morning the family came, Antonio and Rosa and Mama. Mama just cried. Rosa came up to me and her hands touched mine through the wire screen that separated me from the visiting room.

"Oh, Juan. I told you not to go to the party."

"You were right, Rosa."

Her fingers were cool against mine. She's so pretty, I thought, so much prettier than any of those girls last night. I didn't like to see her crying for me.

"But if I hadn't gone," I said, "look what might have happened. You know what Switch would have done to that girl."

"I don't care." She sobbed. "I don't care. . . ."

She walked away from me, over to Mama. Antonio came up. All the time Rosa had been with me, he'd just hung back, watching.

"I hope you're satisfied, Juan," he said. "My cousin. My own cousin."

I just stared at him.

"They're holding Switch for trial," he said. "I suppose you know that, don't you, Juan?"

I shook my head. Besides, I thought, even if they were, it was a good thing. If you were bad, like Switch, you shouldn't be left loose to hurt other people.

"We take you in," Antonio said. "We give you a home. Because you're family." He spat on the floor. "A wetback rat, that's what you are, butting in on things you don't know anything about."

His eyes weren't Antonio's eyes at all. They were ugly, as if he really hated me, as if he'd have killed me if he got the chance.

"You squealed," he said. "You better be glad they're deporting you, Juan. You better be glad they're shipping you back to Mexico. Because if you stayed here, you wouldn't live very long. You know that, don't you?"

The only thing that meant anything to me, at the time he spoke to me, was what he'd said about them deporting me. I believed him. It was what I'd been sure would happen, ever since the police had caught me.

"I'm sorry," I said. "I'm sorry if I caused any trouble."

He started to walk away, then swung around and came right up to the wire screen.

"The jacket," he said. "You give it back, right now, you hear? Why'd I ever let you wear it, you—"

I took the jacket off. It made me feel real bad, not having it any more, even if it was faded and torn and with the new big slit in the elbow where Switch had cut it the night before.

"Just drop it on the floor," my cousin said. "I want to be sure you don't have it when they take you back."

I let the jacket fall. I wanted to try to explain, but I

couldn't. I didn't know the customs and besides, even if I had known them, maybe I still couldn't have explained. It looked, now, as if Antonio would rather have let Switch have the girl. I couldn't understand.

I looked over his head at Rosa. She had stopped crying and was standing very stiff, as if braced against tears. She waved to me when the guards came up and led me away.

"*Adiós,* Juan," she said.

Not "*hasta la vista* . . . until we meet again . . ." but the formal, final good-bye.

"*Adiós,* Rosa."

She was gone when the truck with the bars in it picked us up, me and some other Mexicans who had come across the border for the harvest. The truck was headed for the border. It had no windows, but the guards let me go to the back and stare out through the heavy screens, at the freeway behind me and the great tall buildings and the city, sleepy now in the early morning, the great, beautiful city I knew I'd never see again.

MURDER BETWEEN FRIENDS

by Nedra Tyre

Over their midmorning coffee Mrs. Harrison and Mrs. Franklin settled down to discuss how they were going to murder their landlord, Mr. Shafer. The day before, they had decided that murdering him was the only sane thing to do.

"I believe I'll have a little more sugar for my coffee, please, Matilda," Mrs. Franklin said. At this late date, she was seventy-six, there was nothing she could do about her sweet tooth. "These are the best cheese straws I've ever put in my mouth. You've got to be a born cook to have them turn out this way. Time and again I've followed your recipe exactly, but mine aren't anything like these."

Mrs. Harrison beamed. It was a pleasure to give a little treat to such an amiable person as Mary Sue Franklin, a friend ever since the second grade.

They ate cheese straws and sipped coffee, then wiped their mouths daintily and got down to the business of Mr. Shafer's murder.

"Well, we can't do it with a gun, that's for sure," Mrs. Harrison said. "A gun scares me to death just to look at it. I couldn't bring myself to pull the trigger. Besides, where on earth would we get one? You have to have a permit to buy one and a license to shoot it."

"No, a gun is out," Mrs. Franklin agreed. Then she

sighed. "You read a lot about murder, but when you come right down to it, it's hard to plan one."

Even as they talked they could hear Mr. Shafer thundering like a minotaur up and down the halls looking for his next victim.

"I'll take another cheese straw, Matilda, and then I've got to go to the store. Can I get anything for you? I'll be glad to."

"No, thank you, Mary Sue. But tomorrow we've got to get down to brass tacks. Mr. Shafer gets meaner every day."

They finished their coffee. Mrs. Franklin offered to wash up, but Mrs. Harrison wouldn't hear of it. So Mrs. Franklin went back down the hall to her own tiny room and kitchenette to get her shopping bag. She bumped right into Mr. Shafer, who was coming up the back stairway.

"What you old biddies been yakking about today?" he boomed out at her. "Are you planning to overthrow the government?"

Mrs. Franklin liked banter. A woman never got too old to do a bit of discreet, ladylike flirting. But no light exchange was possible with Mr. Shafer. She smiled her sweetest smile and gave a little bow. "No, my dear," she said in the most genteel conversational tone, "we've been trying to decide how to murder you."

Mr. Shafer paid no attention. He never did pay any attention to what anyone said. "Damned old biddies," he muttered, and stalked on past. "Why is the world so cluttered up with old women?"

He turned out the little glowworm of a light in that part of the hall. He slammed a door somewhere. Even the house shuddered; and he had no business being there at all. The place had belonged to his wife and when she had died it had been willed to their daughter, but Mr. Shafer made the daughter so miserable that she'd left after one of his scenes. Then he had taken over everything.

The next morning the old friends talked again about murdering Mr. Shafer.

Mrs. Franklin asked, as usual, for more sugar for her coffee. She told Mrs. Harrison that was the best apple pie she'd ever eaten.

"It's the cinnamon that makes the difference, that's all," Mrs. Harrison said modestly, "and a little lemon juice."

They finished their snack. They wiped their mouths delicately.

"Well, we can't poison Mr. Shafer," Mrs. Harrison said. "What do we know about poison?"

"We could learn," Mrs. Franklin answered.

"How could we learn, Mary Sue? If we go to the library and ask for books on poison, they're sure to remember us. I know all the staff there. Anyway, when you buy poison the clerk keeps a record of it. The police could trace it straight to us."

Over their chocolate cake the next day, Mrs. Franklin said, "We certainly can't drown him." She was so enmeshed in the cake that she wore a chocolate mustache and for the first time since they'd talked of murder she looked a bit sinister.

"No, I guess we can't drown him. There's no deep water anywhere but in the lake at the city park, and how could we get Mr. Shafer there?"

"He wouldn't go with us. He hates women."

"He hates everybody."

On Thursday when they had finished their pineapple upside-down cake neither of them had any suggestion about how to kill Mr. Shafer.

"I feel so inept and inane, Mary Sue. We've got heads on our shoulders. It looks like we ought to be able to figure out something."

"Maybe we can tomorrow." Mrs. Franklin sounded optimistic.

"What about an axe?" Mrs. Harrison said the next day when they'd eaten every crumb of their cheese cake. "I woke up last night and it came to me as plain as day. Why not an axe?" Her eyes brightened.

"Too messy," Mrs. Franklin said. "We'd ruin our clothes and even if we burned them the police would find the buttons and know they belonged to us."

"I don't mean chop him up," Mrs. Harrison said in alarm that her old friend had thought her capable of such an atrocity. "I just mean hit him on the head with it."

"But we don't have an axe, and if we bought one at the hardware store they'd be sure to remember and report it to the police."

"Now listen, Mary Sue, we've got to put on our thinking caps. We've got to figure out something soon. Mr. Shafer put poor Mrs. Grove out day before yesterday because she wouldn't get rid of her cat, and last night he made Mr. Floyd leave because he said he wheezed too much with his asthma."

"Well, have you thought of a way, Matilda?"

"No, I haven't, Mary Sue. But we will. I just know we will. While we're stuck about a method, there're still lots of other things we could be working on. We've got to figure out when the best time to do it will be. In a rooming house full of people we'll have to draw up some kind of time scheme so no one will be around to see us."

They spent a week devising a time schedule, snooping on the coming and going of the other tenants.

They didn't seem to doubt that they would succeed in their plan. They talked as if their murder was over and done with.

"It's sort of sad," Mrs. Harrison said. "Not a soul in this world will mourn Mr. Shafer."

"Not a tear will be shed for him," Mrs. Franklin said.

"Do you think we ought to send flowers to the funeral?"

"Good gracious, Matilda, I never once thought of that. I just don't know."

"Why not chip in together and send a potted lily? A big floral offering might look like gloating."

"Of course we've got to go to the service."

"Yes, we'll have to or the rest of the people in the house might get suspicious. But don't you think it would look better if we sat more toward the back of the church than the front?"

"I believe about midway would be the best."

"I've thought of it, Matilda," Mrs. Franklin said when she was on her second piece of pecan pie. "It's simple. I'm surprised we haven't thought of it before. Can't you guess?"

"Surely it's not any of the ways we've already talked about."

"Of course not. We couldn't use any of them. We'd be caught red-handed."

"Well, I just don't know. I hate to seem stupid, but I can't even make a good guess."

"A push."

"A push?"

"Yes, just shove Mr. Shafer down the stairs. The basement steps are steep and dark and he goes down there like clockwork every day at eleven. We could take him by surprise. Reach for the small of his back, or use a broom or a mop and give him a shove. The world would be rid of one of the meanest men who ever drew breath."

"Any day at eleven will do?"

"Yes, any day except Sunday, of course. We go to church at eleven then. We couldn't do it on Sunday. I've no intention of missing church just to do away with Mr. Shafer." Mrs. Franklin was flushed over having found their solution. It made her prettier than ever, almost childlike in appearance. No one would have believed that she had been seventy-six on January ninth.

"I've just thought of something, Mary Sue. That man, Mr. Allen, who moved in last week. He never leaves the place. He'd be here at eleven."

"He's no threat," Mrs. Franklin said. "He's hard of hearing. Besides, he's so engrossed in painting that nothing could budge him out of his room except an earthquake."

"Well, then, we'd better get it over with as soon as we can."

"The sooner the better," Mrs. Franklin said.

Of course, they didn't mean it.

Or did they?

They longed for nerve enough to murder Mr. Shafer, but really they couldn't say boo to a goose. Mr. Shafer was mean, he was surly, he made them miserable, exactly as he made everyone else miserable. They wished they could just move out and be rid of him that way, but they'd looked and looked and couldn't find anything for what they could pay; anyhow, they liked living where they were, near stores, near their church, near their doctor's office. They loved the old neighborhood, though it had deteriorated from family dwellings to rooming houses. If only they could get rid of Mr. Shafer and his cruelty. But they couldn't. They had just been whistling in the dark with all their talk of murder. They had just been playing with their imagination. It was their game, as if they were two bettors talking about winning a fortune when they didn't have a dollar between them to place on a horse.

Spring came the very next morning after Mrs. Franklin and Mrs. Harrison had decided that a push was the proper way to murder Mr. Shafer. They couldn't ignore the first warm day of spring. They postponed their usual morning coffee until afternoon. Mrs. Harrison said that she was heading for town to see what the new hats looked like, not that she could buy one. Mrs. Franklin sauntered off to see the daffodils and crocuses in the park.

Mr. Shafer heard them leave. "Darned old harpies," he said. "Maybe I can draw a deep breath with them out of the way for a little while."

The only other person in the house then was Lawrence Allen, who lived in the room next to Mrs. Franklin. But he didn't hear the women go out even though the walls were thin. He couldn't hear very well. He didn't mind that he was growing deaf and that people had to shout at him. Nothing mattered so long as he kept his sight and could lift his right hand to paint. He had waited all his life to paint. He had refused to be a

Sunday painter or an after-working-hours painter. Dabbling hadn't been for him. He had to be a dedicated painter every waking moment. Now that his youth and middle age and all their responsibilities were over he could try to be a painter. He had supported his parents, then his own family; his wife was dead and his two sons were grown and with almost-grown children of their own. After a lifetime of meeting obligations, Allen owed nothing to anyone but himself. All he needed was a place to paint and painting material. He could get by on one meal a day. Nothing was going to stop him from painting, and after months of looking for a place with a proper light, and one that he could afford on his social security, he had found it. Life in one small room with one scanty meal was paradise.

He had just stretched a canvas and had picked up a brush when the door to his room flew open. Mr. Shafer filled the doorway.

"What in hell's going on in here? What's that stink?"

Even Allen's defective ears were outraged by Shafer's bellow.

"Get that muck out of here. This is a bedroom, not a workshop. I won't have it. I tell you I won't have it. It smells like a pigsty. It looks like a garbage dump. I had no idea this was going on. Get this damned junk out of here at once."

He stalked out of the room and walked down the hall. Allen dropped his brush. His hands jerked, his throat grew dry. He ran after Shafer.

"But you can't do this to me, Mr. Shafer. I've waited all my life to paint. I looked all over town for a room with a good light. You can't make me give it up. I won't go." His voice was a shriek. The dark, empty halls boomed with his shouted despair.

Shafer lumbered down the rear stairway. He shouted back to Allen, "I've told you once and for all. You and that damned muck have got to get out of here."

Allen pursued him, entreating him to change his mind. Allen was distraught. He was possessed. He had to convince the man. He couldn't be put out. He couldn't. He wouldn't be. He babbled. He yelled. "Listen to me, Mr. Shafer. You've got to listen."

The emotion in Allen's voice made Shafer turn around. "Get your muck out of here or I'll—" He didn't finish his threat. What he saw on Allen's face terrified him. He ran toward the back porch and, when he had reached it, he slammed the back door in Allen's face. He charged toward the steep basement stairs. It was exactly eleven o'clock—the time that Mrs. Franklin and Mrs. Harrison had decided would be the safest in which to murder him—when he rushed to descend the stairs, but fear over what he had seen on Allen's face made him falter. His foot missed the first step. He stumbled and sprawled.

Lawrence Allen didn't hear the fall. He was weak with rage and numb from the violence he had felt toward Shafer. But the slammed door had brought his sanity back. Thank God, he was in control of himself now. There was no telling what he might have done if Shafer hadn't shut the door. Allen walked back upstairs. He picked his brush up from the floor and began to paint. It steadied him, brought back his purpose and his optimism. Somehow or other he believed he would find a way to keep his room.

After Mr. Shafer's death, Mrs. Harrison and Mrs. Franklin didn't have much to talk about to each other. It was as if they'd talked themselves out in planning Mr. Shafer's murder. Mr. Shafer's pleasant daughter came back and took over the house. It was a happy place then. Mrs. Grove and her cat returned, and Mr. Floyd and his asthma. Mr. Shafer's daughter didn't mind Mr. Allen's painting. In fact, she encouraged him, even sat for him. It wasn't any time before he had two pictures accepted for the Annual State Exhibit.

Mary Sue Franklin and Matilda Harrison were still devoted friends, but a bit miffed with each other. Sometimes Mrs. Harrison's blood boiled a little. Accidental death, her foot, let the poor benighted police think that if they chose. But, of course, Mary Sue Franklin had

done it. Mary Sue's lie didn't fool Mrs. Harrison at all
—she hadn't gone to the park that day. She'd sneaked
back the moment Mrs. Harrison had turned her back
and she'd shoved Mr. Shafer down the stairs at eleven
o'clock, just the way they'd planned.

As for Mrs. Franklin, she was put out because the
method of the murder had been something she'd worked
out all by herself, with no help from Matilda Harrison,
yet Matilda had gone ahead with it all by herself, as if
it had been her own idea. Mrs. Franklin had thought
Mrs. Harrison was shy. She was surprised that Matilda
had turned out to be the pushy type—not that she meant
to make a pun. Well, that just proved that you never
could tell about anyone, not even your best friend.
Imagine, saying she was going to town to look at new
hats, when all the time she had been hiding in the back
hall waiting to shove Mr. Shafer to Kingdom Come.

The old friends kept on having their morning coffee
together, but they were careful not to turn their backs on
each other, and when they looked straight into each
other's eyes, each was dead sure she saw a murderer.

GOOD FOR THE SOUL

by Lawrence Block

In the morning, Warren Cuttleton left his furnished room on West Eighty-third Street and walked over to Broadway. It was a clear day, cool, but not cold, bright but not dazzling. At the corner, Mr. Cuttleton bought a copy of *The Daily Mirror* from the blind newsdealer who sold him a paper every morning and who, contrary to established stereotype, recognized him by neither voice nor step. He took his paper to the cafeteria where he always ate breakfast, kept it tucked tidily under his arm while he bought a sweet roll and a cup of coffee, and sat down alone at a small table to eat the roll, drink the coffee, and read *The Daily Mirror* cover to cover.

When he reached page three, he stopped eating the roll and set the coffee aside. He read a story about a woman who had been killed the evening before in Central Park. The woman, named Margaret Waldek, had worked as a nurse's aide at Flower Fifth Avenue Hospital. At midnight her shift had ended. On her way home through the park, someone had thrown her down, assaulted her, and stabbed her far too many times in the chest and abdomen. There was a long and rather colorful story to this effect, coupled with a moderately grisly picture of the late Margaret Waldek. Warren Cuttleton read the story and looked at the grisly picture.

And remembered.

The memory rushed upon him with the speed of a rumor. A walk through the park. The night air. A knife —long, cold—in one hand. The knife's handle moist with his own urgent perspiration. The waiting, alone in the cold. Footsteps, then coming closer, and his own movement off the path and into the shadows, and the woman in view. And the awful fury of his attack, the fear and pain in the woman's face, her screams in his ears. And the knife, going up and coming down, rising and descending. The screams peaking and abruptly ending. The blood.

He was dizzy. He looked at his hand, expecting to see a knife glistening there. He was holding two-thirds of a sweet roll. His fingers opened. The roll dropped a few inches to the tabletop. He thought that he was going to be sick, but this did not happen.

"Oh, God," he said, very softly. No one seemed to hear him. He said it again, somewhat louder, and lit a cigarette with trembling hands. He tried to blow out the match and kept missing it. He dropped the match to the floor and stepped on it and took a very large breath.

He had killed a woman. No one he knew, no one he had ever seen before. He was a word in headlines— fiend, attacker, killer. He was a murderer, and the police would find him and make him confess, and there would be a trial and a conviction and an appeal and a denial and a cell and a long walk and an electrical jolt and then, mercifully, nothing at all.

He closed his eyes. His hands curled up into fists, and he pressed his fists against his temples and took furious breaths. Why had he done it? What was wrong with him? Why, why, why had he killed?

Why would *anyone* kill?

He sat at his table until he had smoked three cigarettes, lighting each new one from the butt of the one preceding it. When the last cigarette was quite finished, he got up from the table and went to the phone booth. He dropped a dime and dialed a number and waited until someone answered the phone.

"Cuttleton," he said. "I won't be in today. Not feeling well."

One of the office girls had taken the call. She said that it was too bad and she hoped Mr. Cuttleton would be feeling better. He thanked her and rang off.

Not feeling well! He had never called in sick in the twenty-three years he had worked at the Bardell Company, except for two times when he had been running a fever. They would believe him, of course. He did not lie and did not cheat and his employers knew this. But it bothered him to lie to them.

But then it was no lie, he thought. He was not feeling well, not feeling well at all.

On the way back to his room he bought *The Daily News* and *The Herald Tribune* and *The Times*. *The News* gave him no trouble, as it too had the story of the Waldek murder on page three, and ran a similar picture and a similar text. It was harder to find the stories in *The Times* and *The Herald Tribune;* both of those papers buried the murder story deep in the second section, as if it were trivial. He could not understand that.

That evening he bought *The Journal American* and *The World Telegram* and *The Post*. *The Post* ran an interview with Margaret Waldek's half-sister, a very sad interview indeed. Warren Cuttleton wept as he read it, shedding tears in equal measure for Margaret Waldek and for himself.

At seven o'clock, he told himself that he was surely doomed. He had killed and he would be killed in return.

At nine o'clock, he thought that he might get away with it. He gathered from the newspaper stories that the police had no substantial clues. Fingerprints were not mentioned, but he knew for a fact that his own fingerprints were not on file anywhere. He had never been fingerprinted. So, unless someone had seen him, the police would have no way to connect him with the murder. And he could not remember having been seen by anyone.

He went to bed at midnight. He slept fitfully, reliving every unpleasant detail of the night before—the footsteps, the attack, the knife, the blood, his flight from the park. He awoke for the last time at seven o'clock, woke at the peak of a nightmare with sweat streaming from every pore.

Surely there was no escape if he dreamed those dreams night after endless night. He was no psychopath; right and wrong had a great deal of personal meaning to him. Redemption in the embrace of an electrified chair seemed the least horrible of all possible punishments. He no longer wanted to get away with the murder. He wanted to get away *from* it.

He went outside and bought a paper. There had been no developments in the case. He read an interview in *The Mirror* with Margaret Waldek's little niece, and it made him cry.

He had never been to the police station before. It stood only a few blocks from his rooming house but he had never passed it, and he had to look up its address in the telephone directory. When he got there, he stumbled around aimlessly looking for someone in a little authority. He finally located the Desk Sergeant and explained that he wanted to see someone about the Waldek killing.

"Waldek," the Desk Sergeant said.

"The woman in the park."

"Oh. Information?"

"Yes," Mr. Cuttleton said.

He waited on a wooden bench while the Desk Sergeant called upstairs to find out who had the Waldek thing. Then the Desk Sergeant told him to go upstairs where he would see a Sergeant Rooker. He did this.

Rooker was a young man with a thoughtful face. He said yes, he was in charge of the Waldek killing, and just to start things off, could he have name and address and some other details?

Warren Cuttleton gave him all the details he wanted.

Rooker wrote them all down with a ball-point pen on a sheet of yellow foolscap. Then he looked up thoughtfully.

"Well, that's out of the way," he said. "Now what have you got for us?"

"Myself," Mr. Cuttleton said. And when Sergeant Rooker frowned curiously, he explained, "I did it. I killed that woman, that Margaret Waldek, I did it."

Sergeant Rooker and another policeman took him into a private room and asked him a great many questions. He explained everything exactly as he remembered it, from beginning to end. He told them the whole story, trying his best to avoid breaking down at the more horrible parts. He only broke down twice. He did not cry at those times, but his chest filled and his throat closed and he found it temporarily impossible to go on.

Questions—

"Where did you get the knife?"

"A store. A five-and-ten."

"Where?"

"On Columbus Avenue."

"Remember the store?"

He remembered the counter, a salesman, remembered paying for the knife and carrying it away. He did not remember which store it had been.

"Why did you do it?"

"I don't know."

"Why the Waldek woman?"

"She just . . . came along."

"Why did you attack her?"

"I wanted to. Something . . . came over me. Some need, I didn't understand it then, I don't understand it now. Compulsion. I just had to do it!"

"Why kill her?"

"It happened that way. I killed her, the knife, up, down. That was why I bought the knife. To kill her."

"You planned it?"

"Just . . . hazily."

"Where's the knife?"

"Gone. Away. Down a sewer."

"What sewer?"

"I don't remember. Somewhere."

"You got blood on your clothes. You must have, she bled like a flood. Your clothes at home?"

"I got rid of them."

"Where? Down a sewer?"

"Look, Ray, you don't third-degree a guy when he's trying to confess something."

"I'm sorry. Cuttleton, are the clothes around your building?"

He had vague memories, something about burning. "An incinerator," he said.

"The incinerator in your building?"

"No. Some other building, there isn't any incinerator where I live. I went home and changed, I remember it, and I bundled up the clothes and ran into another building and put everything in an incinerator and ran back to my room. I washed. There was blood under my fingernails, I remember it."

They had him take off his shirt. They looked at his arms and his chest and his face and his neck.

"No scratches," Sergeant Rooker said. "Not a mark, and she had stuff under her nails, from scratching."

"Ray, she could have scratched herself."

"Mmmm. Or he mends quick. Come on, Cuttleton."

They went to a room, fingerprinted him, took his picture, and booked him on suspicion of murder. Sergeant Rooker told him that he could call a lawyer if he wanted one. He did not know any lawyers. There had been a lawyer who had notarized a paper for him once, long ago, but he did not remember the man's name.

They took him to a cell. He went inside, and they closed the door and locked it. He sat down on a stool and smoked a cigarette. His hands did not shake now for the first time in almost twenty-seven hours.

Four hours later Sergeant Rooker and the other policeman came into his cell. Rooker said, "You didn't kill that woman, Mr. Cuttleton. Now why did you tell us you did?"

He stared at them.

"First, you had an alibi and you didn't mention it. You went to a double feature at Loew's Eighty-third, the cashier recognized you from a picture and remembered you bought a ticket at 9:30. An usher also recognized you and remembers you tripped on your way to the men's room and he had to give you a hand, and that was after midnight. You went straight to your room, one of the women lives downstairs remembers that. The fellow down the hall from you swears you were in your room by one and never left it and the lights were out fifteen minutes after you got here. Now why in the name of heaven did you tell us you killed that woman?"

This was incredible. He did not remember any movies. He did not remember buying a ticket, or tripping on the way to the men's room. Nothing like that. He remembered only the lurking and the footsteps and the attack, the knife and the screams, the knife down a sewer and the clothes in some incinerator and washing away the blood.

"More. We got what must be the killer. A man named Alex Kanster, convicted on two counts of attempted assault. We picked him up on a routine check and found a bloody knife under his pillow and his face torn and scratched, and I'll give three-to-one he's confessed by now, and he killed the Waldek woman and you didn't, so why the confession? Why give us trouble? Why lie?"

"I don't lie," Mr. Cuttleton said.

Rooker opened his mouth and closed it. The other policeman said, "Ray, I've got an idea. Get someone who knows how to administer a polygraph thing."

He was very confused. They led him to another room and strapped him to an odd machine with a graph, and they asked him questions. What was his name? How old was he? Where did he work? Did he kill the

Waldek woman? How much was four and four? Where did he buy the knife? What was his middle name? Where did he put his clothes?

"Nothing," the other policeman said. "No reaction. See? He *believes* it, Ray."

"Maybe he just doesn't react to this. It doesn't work on everybody."

"So ask him to lie."

"Mr. Cuttleton," Sergeant Rooker said, "I'm going to ask you how much four and three is. I want you to answer six. Just answer six."

"But it's seven."

"Say six anyway, Mr. Cuttleton."

"Oh."

"How much is four and three?"

"Six."

He reacted, and heavily. "What it is," the other cop explained, "is he believes this, Ray. He didn't mean to make trouble, he believes it, true or not. You know what an imagination does, how witnesses swear to lies because they remember things wrong. He read the story and he believed it all from the start."

They talked to him for a long time, Rooker and the other policeman, explaining every last bit of it. They told him he felt guilty, he had some repression deep down in his sad soul, and this made him believe that he had killed Mrs. Waldek when, in fact, he had not. For a long time he thought that they were crazy, but in time they proved to him that it was quite impossible for him to have done what he said he had done. It could not have happened that way, and they proved it, and there was no argument he could advance to tear down the proof they offered him. He had to believe it.

Well!

He believed them, he knew they were right and he— his memory—was wrong. This did not change the fact that he remembered the killing. Every detail was still quite clear in his mind. This meant, obviously, that he was insane.

"Right about now," Sergeant Rooker said, perceptively, "you probably think you're crazy. Don't worry about it, Mr. Cuttleton. This confession urge isn't as uncommon as you might think. Every publicized killing brings us a dozen confessions, with some of them dead sure they really did it. You have the urge to kill locked up inside somewhere, you feel guilty about it, so you confess to what you maybe wanted to do deep in your mind but would never really do. We get this all the time. Not many of them are as sure of it as you, as clear on everything. The lie detector is what got to me. But don't worry about being crazy, it's nothing you can't control. Just don't sweat it."

"Psychological," the other policeman said.

"You'll probably have this bit again," Rooker went on. "Don't let it get to you. Just ride it out and remember you couldn't possibly kill anybody and you'll get through all right. But no more confessions. Okay?"

For a time he felt like a stupid child. Then he felt relieved, tremendously relieved. There would be no electrified chair. There would be no perpetual burden of guilt.

That night he slept. No dreams.

That was March. Four months later, in July, it happened again. He awoke, he went downstairs, he walked to the corner, he bought *The Daily Mirror,* he sat down at a table with his sweet roll and his coffee, he opened the paper to page three, and he read about a schoolgirl, fourteen, who had walked home the night before in Astoria and who had not reached her home because some man had dragged her into an alley and had slashed her throat open with a straight razor. There was a grisly picture of the girl's body, her throat cut from ear to ear.

Memory, like a stroke of white lightning across a flat black sky. Memory, illuminating all.

He remembered the razor in his hand, the girl struggling in his grasp. He remembered the soft feel of her frightened young flesh, the moans she made, the incredible supply of blood that poured forth from her wounded throat.

The memory was so real that it was several moments before he remembered that his rush of awful memory was not a new phenomenon. He recalled that other memory, in March, and remembered it again. That had been false. This, obviously, was false as well.

But it could not be false. He *remembered* it. Every detail, so clear, so crystal clear.

He fought with himself, telling himself that Sergeant Rooker had told him to expect a repeat performance of this false-confession impulse. But logic can have little effect upon the certain mind. If one holds a rose in one's hand, and feels that rose, and smells the sweetness of it, and is hurt by the prick of its thorns, all the rational thought in creation will not serve to sway one's conviction that this rose is a reality. And a rose in memory is as unshakable as a rose in hand.

Warren Cuttleton went to work that day. It did him no good, and did his employers no good either, since he could not begin to concentrate on the papers on his desk. He could only think of the foul killing of Sandra Gitler. He knew that he could not possibly have killed the girl. He knew, too, that he had done so.

An office girl asked him if he was feeling well, he looked all concerned and unhappy and everything. A partner in the firm asked him if he had had a physical checkup recently. At five o'clock he went home. He had to fight with himself to stay away from the police station, but he stayed away.

The dreams were very vivid. He awoke again and again. Once he cried out. In the morning, when he gave up the attempt to sleep, his sheets were wet with his perspiration. It had soaked through to the mattress. He took a long, shivering shower and dressed. He went downstairs, and he walked to the police station.

Last time, he had confessed. They had proved him innocent. It seemed impossible that they could have been wrong, just as it seemed impossible that he could have killed Sandra Gitler, but perhaps Sergeant Rooker could lay the girl's ghost for him. The confession, the proof of his own real innocence—then he could sleep at night once again.

He did not stop to talk to the Desk Sergeant. He went directly upstairs and found Rooker, who blinked at him.

"Warren Cuttleton," Sergeant Rooker said. "A confession?"

"I tried not to come. Yesterday, I remembered killing the girl in Queens. I know I did it, and I know I couldn't have done it, but—"

"You're sure you did it."

"Yes."

Sergeant Rooker understood. He led Cuttleton to a room, not a cell, and told him to stay there for a moment. He came back a few moments later.

"I called Queens Homicide," he said. "Found out a few things about the murder, some things that didn't get into the paper. Do you remember carving something into the girl's belly?"

He remembered. The razor, slicing through her bare flesh, carving something.

"What did you carve, Mr. Cuttleton?"

"I . . . I can't remember, exactly."

"You carved 'I love you.' Do you remember?"

Yes, he remembered. Carving "I love you," carving those three words into that tender flesh, proving that his horrid act was an act of love as well as an act of destruction. Oh, he remembered. It was clear in his mind, like a well-washed window.

"Mr. Cuttleton. Mr. Cuttleton, that wasn't what was carved in the girl. Mr. Cuttleton, the words were unprintable, the first word was unprintable, the second word was 'you.' Not 'I love you,' something else. That was why they kept it out of the papers, that and to keep off false confessions, which is, believe me, a good idea. Your memory picked up on that the minute I said it, like the power of suggestion. It didn't happen, just like you never touched that girl, but something got triggered in your head so you snapped it up and remembered it like you remembered everything you read in the paper, the same thing."

For several moments he sat looking at his fingernails while Sergeant Rooker sat looking at him. Then he said, slowly, "I knew all along I couldn't have done it. But that didn't help."

"I see."

"I had to prove it. You can't remember something, every last bit of it, and then just tell yourself that you're crazy. That it simply did not happen. I couldn't sleep."

"Well."

"I had dreams. Reliving the whole thing in my dreams, like last time. I knew I shouldn't come here, that it's wasting your time. There's knowing and knowing, Sergeant."

"And you had to have it proved to you."

He nodded miserably. Sergeant Rooker told him it was nothing to sweat about, that it took some police time but that the police really had more time than some people thought, though they had less time than some other people thought, and that Mr. Cuttleton could come to him any time he had something to confess.

"Straight to me," Sergeant Rooker said. "That makes it easier, because I understand you, what you go through, and some of the other boys who aren't familiar might not understand."

He thanked Sergeant Rooker and shook hands with him. He walked out of the station, striding along like an ancient mariner who had just had an albatross removed from his shoulders. He slept that night, dreamlessly.

It happened again in August. A woman strangled to death in her apartment on West Twenty-seventh Street; strangled with a piece of electrical wire. He remembered buying an extension cord the day before for just that purpose.

This time he went to Rooker immediately. It was no problem at all. The police had caught the killer just minutes after the late editions of the morning papers had been locked up and printed. The janitor did it, the janitor of the woman's building. They caught him and he confessed.

On a clear afternoon that followed on the heels of a rainy morning in late September, Warren Cuttleton came home from the Bardell office and stopped at a Chinese laundry to pick up his shirts. He carried his shirts around the corner to a drugstore on Amsterdam Avenue and bought a tin of aspirin tablets. On the way back to his rooming house he passed—or started to pass—a small hardware store.

Something happened.

He walked into the store in robotish fashion, as though some alien had taken over control of his body, borrowing it for the time being. He waited patiently while the clerk finished selling a can of putty to a flat-nosed man. Then he bought an ice pick.

He went back to his room. He unpacked his shirts— six of them, white, stiffly starched, each with the same conservative collar, each bought at the same small haberdashery—and he packed them away in his dresser. He took two of the aspirin tablets and put the tin in the top drawer of the dresser. He held the ice pick between his hands and rubbed his hands over it, feeling the smoothness of the wooden handle and stroking the cool steel of the blade. He touched the tip of his thumb with the point of the blade and felt how deliciously sharp it was.

He put the ice pick in his pocket. He sat down and smoked a cigarette, slowly, and then he went downstairs and walked over to Broadway. At Eighty-sixth Street he went downstairs into the IRT station, dropped a token, passed through the turnstile. He took a train uptown to Washington Heights. He left the train, walked to a small park. He stood in the park for fifteen minutes, waiting.

He left the park. The air was chillier now and the sky was quite dark. He went to a restaurant, a small diner on Dyckman Avenue. He ordered the chopped sirloin, very well done, with French-fried potatoes and a cup of coffee. He enjoyed his meal very much.

In the men's room at the diner he took the ice pick from his pocket and caressed it once again. So very sharp, so very strong. He smiled at the ice pick and kissed the tip of it with his lips parted so as to avoid pricking himself. So very sharp, so very cool.

He paid his check and tipped the counterman and left the diner. Night now, cold enough to freeze the edge of thought. He walked through lonely streets. He found an alleyway. He waited, silent and still.

Time.

His eyes stayed on the mouth of the alley. People passed—boys, girls, men, women. He did not move from his position. He was waiting. In time the right person would come. In time the streets would be clear except for that one person, and the time would be right, and it would happen. He would act. He would act fast.

He heard high heels tapping in staccato rhythm, approaching him. He heard nothing else, no cars, no alien feet. Slowly, cautiously, he made his way toward the mouth of the alley. His eyes found the source of the tapping. A woman, a young woman, a pretty young woman with a curving body and a mass of jet-black hair and a raw red mouth. A pretty woman, his woman, the right woman, this one, yes, now!

She moved within reach, her high-heeled shoes never altering the rhythm of their tapping. He moved in liquid perfection. One arm reached out, and a hand fastened upon her face and covered her raw red mouth. The other arm snaked around her waist and tugged at her. She was off-balance, she stumbled after him, she disappeared with him into the mouth of the alley.

She might have screamed, but he banged her head on the cement floor of the alley and her eyes went glassy. She started to scream later, but he got a hand over her mouth and cut off the scream. She did not manage to bite him. He was careful.

Then, while she struggled, he drove the point of the ice pick precisely into her heart.

He left her there, dead and turning cold. He dropped the ice pick into a sewer. He found the subway arcade and rode the IRT back to where he had come from, went to his room, washed hands and face, got into bed and slept. He slept very well and did not dream, not at all.

When he woke up in the morning at his usual time, he felt as he always felt, cool and fresh and ready for the day's work. He showered and he dressed and he went downstairs, and he bought a copy of *The Daily Mirror* from the blind newsdealer.

He read the item. A young exotic dancer named Mona More had been attacked in Washington Heights and had been stabbed to death with an ice pick.

He remembered. In an instant it all came back, the girl's body, the ice pick, murder—

He gritted his teeth together until they ached. The realism of it all! He wondered if a psychiatrist could do anything about it. But psychiatrists were so painfully expensive, and he had his own psychiatrist, his personal, and no-charge psychiatrist, his Sergeant Rooker.

But he remembered it! Everything, buying the ice pick, throwing the girl down, stabbing her—

He took a very deep breath. It was time to be methodical about this, he realized. He went to the telephone and called his office. "Cuttleton here," he said. "I'll be late today, an hour or so. A doctor's appointment. I'll be in as soon as I can."

"It's nothing serious?"

"Oh, no," he said. "Nothing serious." And, really, he wasn't lying. After all, Sergeant Rooker did function as his personal psychiatrist, and a psychiatrist was a doctor. And he did have an appointment, a standing appointment, for Sergeant Rooker had told him to come in whenever something like this happened. And it was nothing serious, that too was true, because he knew that he was really very innocent no matter how sure his memory made him of his guilt.

Rooker almost smiled at him. "Well, look who's here," he said. "I should have figured, Mr. Cuttleton. It's your kind of crime, isn't it? A woman assaulted and killed, that's your trademark, right?"

Warren Cuttleton could not quite smile. "I . . . the More girl. Mona More."

"Don't those strippers have wild names? Mona More. As in Mon Amour. That's French."

"It is?"

Sergeant Rooker nodded. "And you did it," he said. "That's the story?"

"I know I couldn't have, but—"

"You ought to quit reading the papers," Sergeant Rooker said. "Come on, let's get it out of your system."

They went to the room. Mr. Cuttleton sat in a straight-backed chair. Sergeant Rooker closed the door and stood at the desk. He said, "You killed the woman, didn't you? Where did you get the ice pick?"

"A hardware store."

"Any special one?"

"It was on Amsterdam Avenue."

"Why an ice pick?"

"It excited me, the handle was smooth and strong, and the blade was so sharp."

"Where's the ice pick now?"

"I threw it in a sewer."

"Well, that's no switch. There must have been a lot of blood, stabbing her with an ice pick. Loads of blood?"

"Yes."

"Your clothes get soaked with it?"

"Yes." He remembered how the blood had been all over his clothes, how he had had to hurry home and hope no one would see him.

"And the clothes?"

"In the incinerator."

"Not in your building, though."

"No. No, I changed in my building and ran to some other building, I don't remember where, and threw the clothes down the incinerator."

Sergeant Rooker slapped his hand down on the desk. "This is getting too easy," he said. "Or I'm getting too good at it. The stripper was stabbed in the heart with an ice pick. A tiny wound and it caused death just about instantly. Not a drop of blood. Dead bodies don't bleed, and wounds like that don't let go with much blood anyhow, so your story falls apart like wet tissue. Feel better?"

Warren Cuttleton nodded slowly. "But it seemed so horribly real," he said.

"It always does." Sergeant Rooker shook his head. "You poor son of a gun," he said. "I wonder how long this is going to keep up." He grinned wryly. "Much more of this and one of us is going to snap."

ACE IN THE HOLE

by Elijah Ellis

Weldon pounded a large fist against the closed apartment door. He called impatiently, "Hey, Jeanne? It's I, Dave Weldon." Still no answer.

Weldon felt badly abused. All right, he was an hour late for his date with Jeanne Dennis. But it wasn't his fault that his managing editor had thrown him a last-minute assignment, just as he was leaving *The Daily Pioneer* city room, earlier that Friday afternoon.

Dave gave a last frustrated bang on the door, and turned away. He started along the musty corridor toward the stairs. "Nuts to all women," he said aloud.

But a puzzled frown crossed his face. He didn't know Jeanne very well. They'd had only a few dates, but she hadn't seem like the type who would get in a huff because a guy was late, not without giving him a chance to explain.

Besides, when he had talked to her on the phone, she had said something about especially wanting to see him this afternoon, something important she wanted to discuss with him. Weldon hesitated at the top of the stairs and looked back along the hallway toward Jeanne's apartment.

He heard a clatter on the stairs. A wizened little man, the building super, was coming up, panting under the weight of a battered vacuum cleaner. He'd been

cleaning the hallway downstairs when Weldon came into
the building a few minutes ago.

"Hi," Weldon said, and stepped back out of the way.

The man came on up the stairs and with a grunt set
the vacuum cleaner down. He mopped his face on his
sleeve. "Don't ever let anybody tell you that cleanin',
and dustin', and vacuumin' ain't hard work."

"Okay," Weldon said. "Listen, did you happen to
see Miss Dennis go out, in the last hour? She's the girl in
apartment twenty-four—"

"Know who she is," the building super snapped.
"And no, I ain't seen her. Why?"

Weldon gnawed at his lower lip. "I was supposed
to have a date with her. But she doesn't answer her
door."

"Ha," the man snorted. "Changed her mind, probably." He looked Weldon up and down. "Can't say I
blame her."

"Yeah, well, I'm kind of worried about her. She
lives there alone and might have had an accident—a
slip in the shower, or something. I was wondering if
you'd mind opening her apartment? Just to be sure
she's—"

Weldon drew a dollar bill out of his pocket. The man
took it and walked to the door of Jeanne Dennis' apartment. He pounded on the door. No answer. He took a
ring of keys from his shirt pocket, found the one he
wanted, inserted it in the lock. Then he turned the
doorknob and gave Weldon a disgusted look. "Door
ain't even locked," he said, and pushed it open.

"I didn't think to try it," Weldon muttered.

He followed the other man into the apartment. He
called, "Jeanne? Anybody home?"

Silence. No one was in the small, comfortably furnished living room. From where he stood Weldon could
see the kitchenette that opened off the living room was
also empty. That just left the bedroom. While the building super watched disapprovingly, Weldon crossed to the
closed bedroom door, rapped once, then opened it.

Jeanne was lying on the bed. She wore slacks and a

frilly summer blouse. Her face was turned away. She appeared to be sleeping.

Then Weldon saw the hilt of the knife protruding from her chest. He made an angry sound. He shut his eyes and shook his head violently.

Behind him the building super asked, "What's the matter?" He came over, looked past Weldon at the figure on the bed. "Oh, lordy," he breathed.

Slowly they entered the room, looked down at the body. "She's dead," Weldon said wonderingly.

"Yeah." The building super's wrinkled face was a sickish white. Then, his eyes narrowing, he backed out of the room, never taking his gaze from Weldon. "Yeah," he repeated. Suddenly he turned, made a dash for the phone on a little table across the living room. He grabbed the phone, dialed the operator, and blurted, "Get me the cops—and hurry!"

Weldon came out of the bedroom. He pulled the door shut, stood there blinking at nothing. Then his eyes focused on the man at the phone. The building super was yelling, "Yeah, that's the address, and yeah, I said murder. Get over here—fast. I think I got the guy who did it."

The words cut through the numbed shock that gripped Weldon. He started for the building super. "What the—are you crazy?"

The little man dropped the phone. His hand darted into his pants pocket, came out with a knife. The blade snapped open. "Keep away from me, mister. Just stay put, or I'll carve you seven ways from Sunday."

Weldon stared at him unbelievingly. "Listen, I didn't—"

"Save it for the cops." The man's left hand moved. A crumpled dollar bill made an arc across the room, landed at Weldon's feet. "And there's your buck."

"Oh, for—" Suddenly Weldon broke off, turned toward the open doorway that led to the kitchenette. He'd heard something from in there, a soft, scraping sound, followed by a click, as if a door had been gently eased shut. Weldon headed that way on the run. He didn't get far. The little building super darted in front of him, wheeled to face him, knife poised and ready, his feet wide-spread.

"One more step, mister, and you get this right in the belly." He meant it.

Weldon stopped, cursing futilely. He was still cursing when, moments later, two uniformed cops burst into the apartment, followed by a pair of plainclothesmen. Then came a man that Weldon knew, Captain Snyder, commander of the city's North Division detective squad.

Weldon brushed by the building super. "Snyder, somebody took off out the service door in the kitchen, just a couple of minutes ago, probably the killer. Get some men—"

"Well, well," the captain said. "If it isn't the pride of *The Daily Pioneer*. What're you doing here?"

Weldon yelled, "I'm trying to tell you—the killer just left, by the service door."

"He's lyin', anyhow," the little building super put in. "There ain't nobody been in here, not since him and me came in, five, ten minutes ago."

Captain Snyder nodded his big, bald head. "There are men covering all the exits, in any case." He turned to one of the plainclothesmen hovering nearby. "Take this gentleman out in the hallway and get his story. Weldon, you sit down on the sofa over there and shut up. I'll be with you in a minute."

The plainclothesman herded the building super out of the apartment. Weldon threw up his hands in disgust, and did as he was told. Sullenly he watched the cops go into their routine, directed by the captain, who seemed to be everywhere at once. The police surgeon bustled in and headed for the bedroom, followed by two morgue attendants carrying a stretcher between them. Captain Snyder came over to Weldon, finally, and stood a moment looking down at the big reporter's ugly face.

"Let's have it," Snyder said.

"Sure you've got time to listen?"

The captain smiled without humor. "Weldon, there are some newspapermen that I like, but you're not one of them. Now start talking."

Weldon did. When he finished, Snyder said, "Uh huh. Very pretty. At least, your story agrees with Jenson's up to a point. He doesn't think you heard anyone going out the service door in the kitchen. Fact, he thinks you put the shiv in the woman yourself. Then you went into this song and dance about how you couldn't get an answer to your knock, when you ran into him on the stairs. He might be right."

Before Weldon could answer, the two morgue attendants shuffled out of the bedroom and on out to the corridor, carrying the sheet-draped stretcher. The doctor came over to Snyder. He wiped his hands on his handkerchief, and said, "Stabbed once. Ordinary kitchen paring knife, with roughly a four-inch blade. The blade penetrated the heart, causing massive damage to the—"

"Okay," Snyder said. "How long ago?"

The doctor looked pained. "How should I know? I forgot to bring my crystal ball with me. I'd say about"—he looked at his watch—"about an hour ago. Right around four o'clock. But that's just my tentative opinion."

Snyder nodded. "Anything else?"

"Ask me after the autopsy." The doctor hesitated. "One thing, I noticed that her nails are very clean, and the nail on the middle finger of her right hand is broken off short. Could be she put up a bit of a struggle, got her claws into whoever killed her. Then, afterwards, the killer had the presence of mind to scrape her nails clean, removing any bits of skin that had collected under her nails. Anyway, I'll check it."

The doctor left. Snyder turned to Weldon. "Take off your shirt and undershirt."

Weldon growled angrily. But he stripped to the waist. There wasn't a mark on his hairy torso. "Satisfied?" he quipped sarcastically.

The captain shrugged. "Not especially. You know what really sticks in my craw? This little tidbit of yours, about hearing the service door easing shut in the kitchen. Of course, it might be an honest mistake, but . . ."

Weldon ran his hands over his hair. "All I can tell you is what I heard. That little jerk, Jenson, stopped me before I could check on it. But there is a door from the kitchen into the bathroom, and another door from the bath into the bedroom. Neither of us thought to look into the bathroom. The killer could have been in there, hiding. Then when he got the chance, he just eased on out through the kitchen door into the corridor, took off down the back stairs and out of the building."

"Fine," Synder said. He lit a cigarette, inhaled deeply. "Except, just why should this mysterious killer hang around here in the apartment for almost an hour after killing the woman? The woman died around four. Some forty-five minutes later, according to your story, you were out there in the corridor, pounding on the door, and the door wasn't locked. Any second you might have opened it and come inside—"

"I didn't think to try it."

"So you said. Anyway, all this time, the killer is calmly sitting in here. You go away, and a few minutes later you're back, with the building super. The two of you come in and blunder around. And still the killer is here. Then, finally, he leaves." The captain grimaced. "How about it, Weldon?"

Weldon sighed. "Yeah. I guess I must have been mistaken. About that, I mean."

A member of the physical-evidence squad came into the living room, holding a tiny cellophane envelope in one hand, and two white shirts on hangers in the other.

"Captain? Couple of goodies here." He extended the little envelope. "This is a piece of fingernail, probably the one torn from the dead girl's hand. There appear to be traces of blood on it. We'll know more when we get it downtown to the lab."

"Good. What's with the shirts?"

The detective shrugged. "Hanging in the closet in there. Men's shirts, size sixteen and a half, got a laundry mark on them. We—"

"Wait a minute," Weldon said. He leaned forward, stared at a small patch on the sleeve of one of the shirts. Then, with shaky hands, he grabbed the shirts, looked at the laundry marks inside the collars. "Oh, no."

The other two men stared curiously.

Weldon gulped, "Those are mine."

"The captain spoke up, "I take it you knew the lady a little better than you told me."

"No," Weldon shook his head violently. "I swear I didn't bring these shirts here. Last time I saw them, they were hanging in my closet at home. I swear—"

"Don't bother," Snyder said. "In fact, get out of here. I'm tired of looking at you, tired of listening to all this hooey you're putting out. I'll see you later."

Weldon headed for the front door. The cops stood around the living room, silently, watching him go. They reminded Weldon of a bunch of hungry dogs eying a big, juicy bone.

Downstairs, he went along the corridor toward the building entrance. A cop was in the lobby, talking with Jenson. Weldon went past them. Neither man spoke to him, but the building super gave him a dirty look. Weldon returned it, with interest.

He thought about Jenson as he got into his old coupe, and drove away. Handy man with a knife, Jenson was. Just suppose, now, that the dried-up little building super had killed Jeanne Dennis, for some reason of his own. And later, when Weldon showed up, he'd decided to try framing the reporter for the murder. Something to consider.

But that didn't explain how two of Weldon's shirts got into the dead woman's bedroom closet. And it didn't explain the sound of the service door closing, in the kitchen—and Weldon was sure he'd heard that, no matter what he'd said to Captain Snyder.

Weldon turned onto one of the main traffic arteries leading into the downtown district.

"Of course, there could have been two of them, Jenson and someone else, in on it," Weldon muttered aloud. But why would the other person hang around the apartment for an hour, after Jeanne was dead? Looking for something? His mind felt like the rusty insides of a discarded clock. He spotted a bar up ahead, pulled to the curb in front of it, went inside.

Weldon fired down a quick double shot. Then he went back to the phone booth, called the paper, and gave the bare bones of the story to a rewrite man. He'd flesh it out later. *The Pioneer* was an afternoon paper, and the last edition for the day had hit the street more than an hour ago. Tomorrow's first edition wouldn't come off the presses till noon.

When he'd finished, the rewrite man told him, "Brand's here, wants to talk to you. Hold on a second."

Weldon's shaggy eyebrows lifted. Peter Brand, the managing editor, wasn't in the habit of hanging around the city room, once the paper had been put to bed for the day, unless something big was stirring.

"Dave? Where've you been, and what's going on?" The editor didn't sound happy. "We've been getting rumbles here for the last hour, that you're messed up with a killing."

Weldon sighed. He told Brand what had happened.

The editor groaned, "Oh, brother, what *The Times* will do with this!" There was an edge of ice in his voice now. "I don't see any help for it. Have your dinner and come on down here. I'll stay around. And, Dave?"

"Yeah?"

"Keep your mouth shut, if anybody from *The Times* spots you. Much less any of the TV or radio boys—" Brand hung up.

Swearing under his breath, Weldon slammed out of the booth. He beckoned to the bartender. "Bring me a bottle and a glass." He leaned his elbows on the bar, stared down into his refilled glass. He didn't see any answers there.

What did he know about Jeanne Dennis? Very little, really. He'd met her about two weeks ago, at a cocktail party, held in a suite of rooms at one of the big down-town hotels. The host was the congressman for this district, and the nominal guests were the city's news-papermen, radio and TV representatives, a few local politicians, and anybody else who cared to wander in for free booze and sandwiches.

Weldon went only because his editor, Peter Brand, had insisted on it. Brand and his wife were also there, since the editor and the congressman were personal friends. After awhile the party had degenerated into the usual shambles. Weldon had begun a slow but sure movement toward the front door.

Then a laughing voice at his elbow said, "Hello, Mr. Weldon. You want out, too?"

Weldon blinked down at a woman he'd never seen before. She was worth blinking at. "Well, I—do I know you?"

"You do now," she said. "I'm Jeanne Dennis. One of my friends over there told me who you were. I wanted to tell you how much I've enjoyed the series of articles you did in the paper."

Weldon coughed uneasily. "Thank you."

He and Jeanne talked a few minutes, almost shout-ing to make themselves heard over the uproar around them. He learned that Jeanne had come to the party with her brother, who was connected with an ad agency that had done work for the congressman. "Frankly," Jeanne said, with a humorous shrug, "I wish I'd stood in bed. This is a madhouse."

On impulse, Weldon asked, "Want to take off? I can drive you home, or . . ."

Jeanne hesitated, looking around the big, noisy, smoke-clogged room. Then she said, "Well, okay."

They edged along the wall to the door of the suite. Weldon looked back into the room. He saw Peter Brand over by the refreshment table, looking toward him, and lifted a hand in farewell. The editor frowned, then turned away.

In the hotel corridor, Weldon said, "Whew, I'm glad

to get out of that. But what about your brother?"

Jeanne gave a pleased little laugh. "Oh, he'll be all right. He'll be fine."

Something in the tone of her voice made Weldon look down at her curiously. But it was none of his business.

She hadn't been in any great hurry to get home, so they had stopped at a drive-in for sandwiches and coffee. From the conversation, Weldon gathered that Jeanne had only been in the city a short time, and that she worked as a secretary in some office building downtown.

"I don't really like it here," she said. "It's all too big, too noisy. I'm strictly a small-town girl."

Glancing at her, Weldon had his private doubts about that. She was certainly no girl. Weldon guessed she was at least thirty, but a well-preserved thirty.

Eventually he took her home, but she didn't ask him in. She did agree, with evident pleasure, to have dinner with him and go to a movie the next evening.

After that, they went out together a couple more times. Jeanne never again mentioned her personal life. In fact, she turned the conversation into other channels, anytime Weldon asked questions about her past life. Not that he'd thought anything of it, at the time, but once or twice, when they were out together, Weldon had thought he saw an expression of sheer boredom cross her pert face fleetingly. But if he bored her, why should she date him? Certainly not for his good looks, or his money. He didn't have much of either.

He had been in her apartment just two times before today. And nothing had happened either time, beyond a little more or less innocent smooching. He most assuredly hadn't left any spare shirts at her place. . . .

That brought it up to this Friday. Jeanne had called him at the paper, to his surprise, and there had been a tinge of excitement in her voice when she asked him to come over for a couple of drinks that afternoon.

But, at the last minute, Pete Brand had sent him out on an assignment. That had taken almost an hour.

So he had arrived at Jeanne's place shortly before five, instead of at four, as he had planned.

Now Weldon squinted at the bottle on the bar in front of him. It was more than half-empty. One more shot, and he'd go on down to *The Pioneer* building and face the music.

The police surgeon had said Jeanne was killed around four o'clock. If he'd got there when he was supposed to, he might have saved her life.

Weldon left the bar and drove downtown to *The Pioneer* building. He put his car in the parking lot beside the building and walked to the front entrance. Dark clouds hung in the early-evening sky, and there was the feel of rain in the air.

Up in the city room on the third floor, he went to the managing editor's glass-walled cubbyhole.

Pete Brand was at his desk, leaning far back in his swivel chair, gazing up at the ceiling. He was a tall, angular man in his late forties, with a long, saturnine face and sleek, black hair touched with gray at the temples. He saw Weldon and said, "Come on in and sit down, Dave."

Weldon took the chair, facing the editor across the wide desk. He lit a cigarette. He was feeling woozy from the whisky and realized he hadn't eaten since morning. He gazed silently at Brand, waiting.

Brand drummed on the desk top. He asked abruptly, "You kill that woman?"

"No, of course not," Weldon told him. "I just dated her a few times. Nothing serious. Actually, I hardly even knew her."

"I see." Brand hummed softly to himself. "Well, I have a man and a photographer out, following up on it. Captain Snyder is playing it close to his vest. The 'expect an arrest shortly, but no statement at this time' routine."

Weldon shifted uncomfortably in his chair. He wondered what Brand was thinking. Nothing good, that was sure.

"Pete, I'm sorry about this," Weldon said. "But it's

just one of those lousy things that happen—"

Brand gave a short bark of laughter. "Yeah, just one of those things. I'm sure my wife will be comforted to know that."

Weldon groaned silently. *The Daily Pioneer* belonged to Brand's wife, Iris, who had inherited it, along with a potful of money, from her father. For all practical purposes, Peter Brand was the boss.

That didn't mean that Iris had no say in what went on. She still had a firm grip on the purse strings, and a firm and profound distaste for anything that might in any way damage her position as one of the city's real social leaders.

Weldon asked quietly, "You want me to quit, or wait for you to fire me?"

Brand kept his eyes on his hands. "For the moment, we'll let it ride." He flicked back the cuff of his shirt and glanced at his watch. "I have to go. We're having guests in tonight."

"Okay." Weldon stood up slowly. "I'll—"

Suddenly Brand burst out, "Haven't you any ideas at all about this? Something the woman may have said to you, some passing reference to another boyfriend, someone she was afraid of—anything at all?"

"No, Pete. There's just nothing."

The editor thrust back his chair, got to his feet. His dark eyes bored into Weldon. "I just wish I could be sure of you, absolutely sure that you had nothing to do with this mess."

"I didn't. For what it's worth, I'll swear to you that I don't know any more about it than you do."

The two left the office, rode down in the elevator and crossed the echoing lobby. Outside, the clouds had thickened in the dark sky. A few drops of rain spattered down as they rounded the corner of the building to the parking lot.

Brand stopped beside his big, shiny sedan. "Where are you going now?" he said, opening the door.

"Home, I guess. Wait for Snyder to come for me with the handcuffs."

"Very funny," the editor said. With a curt nod, he got in his car and a moment later drove out of the lot.

Weldon plodded on to his battered coupe. The rain was falling heavier now. It matched his mood exactly. For a time he drove around town aimlessly. Then he went home, two rooms and bath in a dingy apartment house on the edge of the business district.

He entered the apartment, turned on lights and looked around. He went into the bedroom and opened the closet there. He eyed the shirts hanging on the rod at one end. Two were missing. He had no idea how long they'd been gone.

Turning, he looked across the room at the window in the far wall. The fire escape was just outside, and he never bothered to lock the window. Anyone who wanted to could get in and out.

But why? To make it look like Weldon and Jeanne Dennis were something more than friends, by planting a couple of lousy shirts in her apartment? If the cops accepted the idea that he and Jeanne were lovers, it would—in their minds, at least—give him a strong motive for killing her; jealousy, hate, any one of the other aberrations that supposedly grew out of shady love affairs.

The only thing clear was that the killer knew him, or at least knew about him, and where he lived, and that he and Jeanne had had a few dates. For some reason, he wanted it to look as if Weldon were deeply involved with her, wanted to frame Weldon to take any possible heat off himself.

Weldon wandered around the tiny apartment, trying to see if anything else was missing. As far as he could tell, there wasn't. He was anything but a good housekeeper. A dozen people could have prowled through the apartment, and chances were that he would never know the difference.

He remembered the one time Jeanne had been up here. She had wanted to see where he lived. One look had been enough for her. "What hit this place, a tornado?" she'd laughed. Weldon had muttered some lame excuse, and got her out as quickly as he could.

The whisky he'd had earlier had worn off. His stomach felt queasy, and he was getting a headache. That, at least, he could cure. He found an untapped fifth of bourbon. As he took a drink, the phone rang. Reluctantly, he went out to the living room, picked up the phone. "Yeah?" he said wearily.

"That you, Weldon? Snyder here."

"Great," Weldon said bitterly.

"Take it easy. What's your blood type?"

"Type O. Why?"

"Lucky boy. We'll check that, and if you're lying, you've had it. But—"

Weldon broke in, "Would you mind telling me what you're talking about?"

"That little piece of fingernail the boys found in the Dennis woman's place—it was on the carpet in the bedroom—was her fingernail. There was a speck of blood on it, and a couple of microscopic fragments of skin. Bloodtype AB. Not the woman's blood. So—"

"Did you by any chance think to take a look at that little jerk of a building super, Jenson?"

The captain laughed. "Yeah, as a matter of fact. He didn't like it even a little bit when we told him to start peeling. Not a mark on him—at least, nothing fresh. Besides he's like you, type O."

"Too bad," Weldon said. "What happens now? Have you found Jeanne's brother? I told you about him."

"No, we haven't found him. In fact, I don't think he exists. He doesn't work for the ad agency that handles our congressman's publicity here, or any other agency that we've checked so far."

Weldon pondered that a moment. "I'm beginning to think Jeanne Dennis didn't even exist."

"Funny thing, I agree with you. There wasn't a thing in that apartment, or in the woman's purse, that indicated who she was. No driver's license, no letters, no bills, no nothing, except for a little overnight case we found on a closet shelf that had initials on it. But they weren't 'J.D.', they were 'L.N.' Something else was in that little case—fourteen hundred and some-odd dollars, in cash."

"Oh, brother."

"You aren't out of the woods yet, Weldon, so don't make any sudden plans to leave town." The captain's voice hardened. "But I guess you can get out your typewriter and start knocking out another of your cute little stories about police harassment and general of-ficial stupidity. I enjoyed the last piece you did on the department. I really did."

The captain hung up. Weldon stood there, gazing at the phone in his hand. With a wry smile, he gently put the phone on its cradle and reached for the bottle of bourbon. He was feeling better, in more ways than one. Suddenly he was hungry as a wolf.

He had a quick shower, a shave, and then he dressed and headed out of the apartment. He had his hand on the doorknob when the phone rang again. "Now what?"

He answered the phone, and immediately a scared voice blurted, "This Dave Weldon? Listen, Weldon, I got to see you. Right now."

"Who is this?"

"This is Al Jenson—you know, I seen you this after-noon. I'm sorry about all that. But you got to help me. There ain't nobody else. I can't go to the cops, not now. But—"

"All right, all right. Calm down, Jenson."

"I know who it was, killed that woman. I wasn't sure before—but I am now." He gave something between a laugh and a sob of fear. "I seen this guy two or three times, goin' into this woman's apartment, always late at night. I seen him again this afternoon. He came in the back way and up the back stairs. About four o'clock it was. He didn't know I seen him—"

"Who, Jenson? Who was it?" Weldon shouted ur-gently.

Jenson babbled on as if he hadn't heard. "I knew the guy's name. I made it my business to find out, a few days ago. Thought it might come in handy sometime.

Then, this afternoon when you and me found the woman dead, well, I thought I saw a chance for a bundle. That's why I acted like I did. Stopped you from chasin' the guy when he took off out the kitchen door. Later on, after the cops finally left, I called him, told him we'd better have a talk. He came over to my place about an hour ago. He didn't try to put on no act. Just asked how much I wanted. Then he made me this deal."

Jenson stopped, panting for breath. Weldon didn't speak. He was afraid the man would panic, and hang up. He shifted the phone from one ear to the other. He mopped the sweaty palm of his free hand down his shirt.

Jenson gulped, then went on. "What he wanted, he wanted me to help him knock you off, Weldon. You have something, I don't know what, but something he wants real bad. He's afraid of you, see. I wasn't havin' any of that—no murder raps for me. I told him so, and he pulled a gun on me. He come at me. But I got the door of my place open and run, him right behind me. I got out of the building and took off. Any second I was expectin' him to start blastin', but he didn't. But he was followin' me. I shook him off, finally. At least I think— Weldon, help me."

"Where are you?"

"A phone booth, at a fillin' station two blocks down the street from the apartment buildin'. Corner of Third and Harvey. Come—"

"Who was the man, Jenson? Tell me!"

But Weldon was yelling into a dead phone. For a split second he hesitated, chewing at his lower lip. Then he put down the phone and ran out of the apartment. *Get to Jenson first. Then get in touch with Captain Snyder. But first, get to Jenson.*

Weldon reached the corner of Third and Harvey less than five minutes later. But it might as well have been five years, for all the good it did Al Jenson.

Weldon parked his car, walked toward the milling

crowd of people on the corner in front of the closed service station. A police car was in the driveway, its red roof light blinking on and off. Weldon pushed through the crowd until he could see the telephone booth, the shattered glass of the folding door, and the body sprawled half in, half out of the booth. A uniformed cop was bending over the body.

A man near Weldon was saying excitedly, "Darndest thing I ever saw. Just like a movie, or TV play. I was out on my front porch across the street. I noticed this here car coming along, real slow. It stopped right there at the curb—and pow, pow, pow. Just like that. Then it took off down the street with tires a-screeching. And the feller there, he come tumbling out of the phone booth—"

Weldon didn't wait to hear any more. He went back to his car, got inside. He doubled a fist, and pounded it against the steering wheel. He drove away.

The duty sergeant at the North Division station house told him Captain Snyder had left for the day. Weldon thanked the sergeant, walked out of the ancient building and back to his car. He could probably catch Snyder at home.

He started to drive out to Snyder's place, then realized he didn't know the address. His own apartment was less than a block away, so he went there, dragged up the stairs to the second floor and into the apartment. He found the telephone directory, leafed through it to the 'S' pages.

Jenson had said Weldon had something the killer wanted, wanted desperately, enough to kill for it. Jenson had said a lot of things, but not the killer's name. And without that little item, the rest was useless.

Or was it? Something, evidently some material item, that the killer wanted—something given to him by Jeanne Dennis. Nothing else made any sense. Only Jeanne Dennis had never given him anything.

Weldon looked slowly around the cluttered living room. He remembered again that Jeanne had been up here once. But he had been with her every minute. She'd had no chance to stash anything away. No, wait, not every minute.

She'd said she wanted to go to the bathroom. She had been alone in there.

Weldon hurried into the bedroom, into the adjoining bathroom. He threw aside the soiled laundry in the corner. There was nothing there, or under the rusty iron tub, or behind it, nothing in the medicine chest, except a jumble of shaving gear, toothbrushes and the like, and nothing on the shelf above the tub. That was all there was. It was a good idea while it lasted.

He turned to the door. Then he looked back over his shoulder at the toilet. Feeling slightly silly, he walked over, lifted the lid from the water tank and peered inside. And there it was, submerged in the murky water—a small, plastic-wrapped parcel.

Weldon plunged his arm into the tank, grabbed the package. He tore it open. Inside the first layer of plastic wrapping was another, making it waterproof. Inside the second wrapping was a tightly folded paper, and something else—a gold ring, a wedding ring. Weldon blinked at it laying on his palm. Slowly he unfolded the paper. It was a marriage license, dated ten years ago, in some town in Maryland, halfway across the continent from here.

Weldon read the names written in on the certificate. One was Lola Norris. There had been a bag with the initials 'L.N.' found in Jeanne Dennis' apartment.

Then the other name, the man's name, jumped up and hit Weldon in the face. He sat down suddenly on the toilet seat, staring unbelievingly.

But there it was. "Peter John Brand," he said aloud.

"That's me," said a voice from the open doorway. "No—don't move, Dave. Don't move a muscle."

Weldon looked at the managing editor of *The Pioneer,* at the gun in his hand, back up at his set face. Brand waggled the gun gently.

"You, Pete?" Weldon stammered. "I don't get it."

The muzzle of the gun pointed at Weldon's chest. "Give me that damn paper and ring."

Weldon handed them over and Brand, after a quick glance, shoved them into his jacket pocket. Weldon shook his head dazedly. "But what—?"

"A very simple, sordid little tale," Brand said. "A long time ago, I married a girl named Lola Norris, in Maryland. After about six months, I'd had it with her. I hit the road, but I didn't bother to divorce her. I eventually ended up here. Time went by. If I thought of Lola at all, it was only that she had probably got a divorce.

"I didn't have any trouble getting on with *The Pioneer*. Before long, I was making out pretty well with the boss' daughter. . . ."

Weldon ran a finger around under his collar. Sweat poured down his face. "Then what?"

Brand continued, "I married the dame. The old man conveniently died about that time, and I had it made. But I made it too big. My name as editor of *The Pioneer* got mentioned in other papers. Lola saw my name. As soon as she could con some sucker out of traveling money, here she came. She called herself Jeanne Dennis, but it was my own sweet Lola. She hadn't got a divorce, which made me a bigamist. Can you imagine what my wife would have said to that? I paid Lola off, for a couple months. You can figure the rest. She got greedy, wanted more, and more," he said.

Then Brand gave a twisted smile. "Well, she had to go. But after that cocktail party at the hotel, she told me she had an ace in the hole. I saw her with you that night. So I had to believe her when she said she'd given you a sealed envelope with this marriage license in it, telling you to open it in case anything happened to her—"

Weldon broke in, "She never said a word about anything like that."

Brand sighed. "I know that now, but it's a little late. You can blame Lola—or Jeanne, if you want to call her that."

Brand's finger started to tighten on the trigger.

"Wait a minute!" Weldon yelled. "Let me smoke a cigarette—"

Brand frowned. He lowered the gun slightly. "Okay. Have your cigarette."

Weldon fumbled out his pack, shoved a cigarette between his lips. He managed to light it. His heart was pounding at his ribs like a snare drum. If, just for one instant, Brand would relax his guard—

The editor was saying conversationally, "I talked to Lola on the phone this morning, and she told me she was having you over for a drink later on. I figured she was going to pull something. Probably what it was, she was going to tell you about the little package in your john."

Brand laughed. "Of all the places to hide something! I went over this rat trap from end to end last night when I was here, and got the two shirts. I looked everywhere, except where it was."

"What did you want with those shirts?" Weldon asked.

"Oh, just a little stage setting. I took them to Lola's place this afternoon after I'd sent you off on that wild-goose chase. I put a knife in Lola almost as soon as she opened the door. But not before she clawed my left arm."

He unbuttoned his left cuff, pulled the sleeve up. There were four parallel red scratches along his forearm. Weldon moved slightly, and Brand quickly brought the gun to bear again.

"You ready? Then sit still. I had on a short-sleeved shirt when I went up there. I had to drive all the way home to get this one I'm wearing now. Anyway, I killed her, laid her out on the bed, then waited for you, Dave boy. Even left the door unlocked, so you'd have no trouble getting in. I was going to put a bullet through your temple, then put the gun in your hand, and lay you out alongside Lola. A lover's quarrel, followed by murder and suicide. But then you had to drag that miserable little pipsqueak in with you. So there was nothing

for me to do but get out of there by the back door—
and wait."

"Must have been rough," Weldon said tonelessly.

"Then that Jenson called me, at the office. But I
guess all's well that ends well, huh?"

Weldon tried to moisten dry lips. "You went to see
Jenson, then tailed him when he ran out on you. You
must have lost him long enough for him to call me on
the phone. Then you found him again."

"Something like that. Well, Dave, I hate to do this,
but I really have to be getting home. Iris will be worried. And we can't have that, can we?"

The gun came up, steadied. Weldon knew he was
all out of time. He tensed his muscles for a desperate
lunge. But suddenly Brand was yanked backward. His
arms flew up and he gave a startled squawk. The gun
went off, and the heavy slug tore a hole in the ceiling,
scattering the plaster.

Then Brand was on the floor, his arms behind his
back. Captain Snyder was kneeling on top of him,
briskly snapping handcuffs on the editor's wrists.

Snyder gave Weldon a brief smile. "Sergeant at the
station house said you'd been in looking for me. I had
heard about Jenson being knocked off, thought there
might be some connection, so I drove over to visit. I
came in about five minutes ago, I guess . . ." He ges-
tured at Brand. "This one sure likes to talk, doesn't he?"

Weldon tried to speak, couldn't. He just shook his
head. Finally he managed to say, "You've been here
all that time? Why didn't you—?"

"I wanted to hear what Brand had to say." Again the
captain smiled. "Besides, I didn't think it would hurt
you to sweat a little."

Weldon drew in a deep breath, let it out slowly.
"That's just lovely, Captain." He paused. "You like
steak chased with bourbon?" At the captain's nod,
Weldon said, "Later on, let's have some. I'm buying."

BAD NOOSE

by Arthur Porges

For some mornings now, Major Hugh Morley had risen just after dawn, and by painful, intricate maneuvering, put his broken body into the wheelchair beside the bed. Sitting in it, by the side window, he could watch Goering pass by the house on his way to the little creek.

The name, his own invention, he felt was quite appropriate since the big diamondback rattler was fat, gaudily-clad, and dangerous. Like most wild creatures, the snake had his own routine and territory, to both of which he adhered with great fidelity. Old and wise, nearly five feet long and thick as a man's arm in the middle, with ten large buttons, he had learned to avoid people. If he had to pass the ranchhouse, he came by on the side where nobody was likely to notice him. He was unaware of the watcher overhead, who had been following his movements with secret satisfaction.

The snake had to have water; this had been a dry year, and many wild animals were forced to invade gardens and farms in order to drink. Nor could Goering avoid passing close to the house, since between his den under a rock and the creek was a deep, rugged ravine that would have been troublesome and time-consuming to cross.

"Right on schedule, as usual!" the major muttered one particular morning. He knew that just as punctually the rattler would be returning by the same route in midafternoon—a more risky journey, since people were more apt to be around then. But on these fifty brushy acres, with only Morley, his sister Grace, and his detested brother-in-law Malcolm Lang in residence, traffic was normally light, and Goering had little to fear. The woman would flee at the sight of his thick body, screaming the house down, whereupon the snake could glide into hiding; as for Lang, he was usually so high that if he saw the rattler at all he'd count six of the snakes.

The major had reason to hate his brother-in-law. Lang, while drunk, his usual state, had come down the dirt road from the highway at close to sixty-five the year before, roared into the front yard without slowing noticeably, and hurtled Morley twenty-odd feet through the air into the side of the barn. If the old boards hadn't crumpled under the impact, the victim could not have survived. Now, racked with pain and unable even to get down from the second floor unaided, the major was not convinced that survival was much of a blessing. Before the accident, he had been an active, highly competent sportsman, and the change to a life of contemplative invalidism was hard to take. Naturally, in this irrational world, Lang had escaped with one tiny cut on his forehead; the vehicle was a wreck.

The fellow's drunken criminality was only the last and worst of his acts. By marrying Grace, Lang had crossed things up badly for the major. Both Morley and his sister had inherited many valuable securities from their father, but the major, a speculator by nature, soon lost every penny of his share. He was glad, after that, to live with Grace, who at thirty-two seemed most unlikely ever to find a husband. Morley forgot the power of money. She was big, florid, and quite bovine both in her movements and nature. He found her easy to handle, and had hopes for using her securities to increase the family fortune—until Lang came along. Whether it was the house and inheritance or true love, the major could not prove, but he had his opinion.

However, there was nothing he could do; if a person-
able man wanted Grace, she was only too happy to
accept him, no questions asked. She even thought it was
her destiny to redeem Malcolm from the curse of liquor.
She was an easy victim. Morley's protests could not
prevent Lang from squandering much of her substance,
but at least he was able to slow the process, so that
Malcolm would abuse his wife and drink more as punishment. In most cases, she sided with her husband, except in keeping her brother upstairs.

Morley had two hundred dollars a month from his
insurance company, following the accident, would have
it for life, but since he needed the kind of care which,
if available at any price, would cost a great deal more
than that, he had to stay with somebody. Forced by
circumstances to stay in the same house with the man
who had crippled him, he didn't have to like it, and
his hate grew. He saw Lang mistreating the helpless
Grace, who preferred even a bullying sot to no husband,
drinking himself sodden, and wasting her money—
money that the major felt was partly his responsibility,
even if Dad had left that portion to her.

After some months of this unpleasant existence Morley hit on the idea of murder as a way out of it. If
Lang could be removed permanently, and in such a
way that no suspicion could be directed against his wife
or the major, life would be a good deal more tolerable.
Unable any longer to hunt or fish, Morley could console
himself with the stock market, and—as he honestly believed—build up Grace's fortune, somewhat depleted,
but still sizeable.

But for a broken man confined to a wheelchair, the
murder of an active enemy who keeps his distance can
pose a difficult problem. The major, an expert shot,
could take his rifle and put a soft-nose slug into Lang
at any distance up to three hundred yards, right from
the window, but that meant paying the ultimate penalty
in the gas chamber. No, the idea was to get rid of the
swine and not get caught. That was where Goering came
in. It was just a matter of getting snake and victim to-

gether in the right circumstances, and Morley had that
nicely figured out.

Today would be the day. Grace was driving to town;
Lang was going to stay at home and, unless the major
goofed, would get thoroughly drunk. Morley hoped
Goering had venom in the amount and toxicity implied
by his bulk. If so, Lang would never really know what
was happening; the alcohol would make him die faster
by dilating his vessels and carrying the poison more
quickly through his body. That was important; the
major didn't want the fellow coming to the house, and
maybe leaving a message, one that the killer couldn't get
downstairs to destroy.

When Grace brought up his lunch she said, "I'll be
leaving now, dear. There are extra cookies, in case you
want to make coffee on the hot plate later. If anything
special comes up," she added diffidently, "Malcolm will
be around; just call him."

"Malcolm!" the major boomed, making sure Lang
heard him. "Before you're a mile away that human
sponge will be stinking drunk!"

She winced. "Really, dear, I wish you wouldn't. He's
so very, very sorry about—about everything."

"Hah!" Morley grunted. He patted her big, soft hand.
"Don't worry about me; have a good time in town;
buy the place out!"

After eating with more haste than usual, the major
wheeled himself over to the front window. Sure enough,
Lang came out, carrying a fifth of the best whisky, and
stretched out in the recliner just a few yards from the
house, where the shade of a eucalyptus tree moderated
the heat of the May sun. The first cog had clicked into
place, Morley noted with relief. If his brother-in-law
had decided to drink inside the house, the scheme
would be out for this time.

After downing four quick, big slugs, Malcolm looked
up at the cripple and yelled, "Nobody tells me when
to drink!" His voice already had a furry edge. He didn't
even eat anything, the major told himself gleefully.
The swine'll be out cold in no time.

The prophecy soon became fact. Red-faced, breathing stertorously, Lang lay back in the chair oblivious to the world. It was unlikely that even death in a terrible form would arouse him before stilling his heart forever, or so Morley hoped.

An hour later, Goering came by, returning from water and a hunting expedition by the creek. Sitting at the side window, the major was ready. He had the nine-foot surf-casting pole, which held a twenty-pound nylon line. There was a noose at the end, very carefully made. It had to be tight-running enough to stay open in a loop, but too loose to bind when he tugged on the line.

Goering, he thought, was not quite normal today. The big snake made several unscheduled stops, raising his ominous head uneasily to peer about. Twice he buzzed loudly, and seemed to writhe for no cause. Well, Morley told himself, the more irritable the better.

It took all his skill to manipulate the pole through a window; no chance for a free cast. But the job was different from dropping a tiny fly on the water many yards away. Instead, he landed the noose right in front of the diamondback, which rose angrily, uplifted tail a blur as it rattled. That was the major's opportunity; with an expert flip, he sent the loop over the snake's head to a point about fifteen inches down his length, and drew it tight.

Furious and baffled, the huge rattler fought against the mysterious enemy that gripped him. But Morley didn't dawdle; he worked at the reel, hauling his captive up. This was very ticklish. He had to bring the snake through the wide window, and let him down via the front one—and without getting fanged.

He wheeled back from the sill, gingerly brought the squirming bundle through, turned at right angles, and thrust Goering quickly through the other window. The old boy is heavy, he told himself; must weigh fifteen pounds, at least.

By moving very close to the sill, and using the full length of the pole—luckily his arms were still muscular—Morley was able to lower the diamondback directly

down to the recliner. He took a sobbing breath, suddenly doubtful. If by some miracle Malcolm came to,
or a witness appeared, he could always say it was a
joke—that he was trying to scare the guy, and had no
intention of letting the snake get close enough to strike.
But once Lang was bitten, the major thought, I can
still say it was a joke, but that I goofed; let the reel
get away from me. He remembered the horror of being
hurled through the air, then the weeks of agony, and
the broken body that now plagued him. Lang had it
coming; besides, he wouldn't know what hit him, which
was better than Morley's fate.

Squirming, buzzing, his tongue flashing in and out,
the rattler came to rest on Malcolm's chest. Finding
himself on something firm, the big snake struck with
lightning speed. Twice, three times he hit home at
Lang's neck and face. Angry and bitter as he was, Morley turned pale, and his hands shook. But Malcolm
didn't know much. He pawed drunkenly at his face, as
if plagued by a fly, and relapsed again into a stuporous
sleep. Green-faced, the major let Goering strike once
more. That should be it. Lang looked bad already,
twitching convulsively as the venom spread through his
dilated blood vessels. It was unlikely he would ever
return to consciousness.

Now came the trickiest part. The major had a stick
about a yard long, to which he'd tied a sharp penknife,
blade open. He had to reel the snake up, and then cut
the line where it looped around his middle. Nor could
he kill the thing, since there was no way to credit the
job to Lang. If Malcolm had aroused enough to fall to
the ground, then Morley could have battered the snake,
and dropped it near, along with the stick. But lying
dead in the chair, the victim obviously had not been
able to kill his attacker. Nor could the major pull him
out with a fish hook; no way to release the barbed fly
afterwards. What a giveaway that would be!

Gradually he brought the lashing captive up to the
window. He had to brace the pole against the arm of
his chair, holding it with one hand while he reached out

with the other, aiming the knife blade. But the big rattler gave a sudden powerful snap of its muscular body; the butt of the pole slipped, so that the end dropped abruptly, slapping hard against the sill; and the line broke, dropping Goering to the ground. There, with a foot of nylon trailing from his middle, the snake made a ludicrously hurried departure.

Morley watched, aghast. If anybody found that snake carrying a fish-line belt! Then he relaxed. With the way a snake's belly rubs the ground, the nylon would soon wear through, even if Goering, annoyed, didn't writhe free before then.

Still, he wished he could now get rid of the rest of the line, so no matching could ever take place; but he couldn't ask Grace to hide it, obviously; nor could he get it into the trash for burning, not while immobilized up here. And the stuff didn't burn well, just melted and reeked. No, he was stuck with it, but the risk was minimal; Goering would not be found with the fragment of line.

There was really only one weakness in the whole plan, but that couldn't be helped. Some might wonder whether a snake could bite a man near the face while he was well off the ground. However, the recliner was fairly low, even where the back slanted up, and a big rattler could reach that far. The fact that he wouldn't, particularly if unmolested, was something to be debated, but not subject to absolute proof. More important was the fact that no matter what suspicions might be aroused, both Morley and his sister were in the clear— she, by being far away in town; he through confinement upstairs. The use of a surf rod was a notion too far out to be guessed by the most astute sheriff.

Too bad, the major thought, that I can't spare Grace the shock of discovery. But if I call the police and report Malcolm's death, I'd have to explain how the snake did it, and I'd much rather not risk such a detailed account. Nor can I say he's dead, since that would be hard to tell from up here. So it's up to poor Grace.

Well, she's pretty placid by nature; she'll get over it. He's not much of a loss, I should think.

There was quite a scene when Grace came home and found Malcolm dead and unpleasantly swelled in the chair. But his expression was peaceful; the alcohol had sped him to the grave, but mercifully.

The sheriff, when he came, seemed puzzled by the event. "I can't imagine why a rattler would bite a man lying in a chair, minding his own business—unless Lang teased him by throwing a stone or something. Even then —I dunno." Then his expression grew hard. "But there are too many rattlers in the area this year. We're gonna have a drive day after tomorrow. It suppose it'll be all right if we include your ranch. The Lawsons said okay; and the Wilersons; and the Harpers."

"I don't think—" Morley began hastily, but Grace interrupted.

"Of course," she said. "I just wish you'd had the drive b-before p-poor M-Malcolm—" She was sobbing again.

"You were saying?" the sheriff said, looking at the major.

"I was just thinking poor Grace would rather not have so many people around, yelling and beating the bushes, but—" He shrugged. By the time they found Goering, if they did, the loop would almost certainly be shredded off. In any case, he daren't protest too much.

"Well, that's settled, then," the sheriff said. "Guess that's all for now."

As he drove off, Morley looked pensive; but after a few moments he brightened. The man didn't suspect anything, that was obvious; he was just a little disturbed by the unusual circumstances. As for the hunt, it was too bad Grace had given permission so fast. While they would undoubtedly kill a lot of rattlers—and plenty of harmless reptiles, too—the sage veterans like Goering would be well down in their dens, and safe. Not that the diamondback would drag a line for more than twenty-four hours; before the hunt began, the incriminating bit of nylon would be just debris in the brush.

About three on the afternoon of the great snake drive, the crowd of men and youths reached the Lang ranch. Most of them were armed with hoes, flails, and clubs, but a few of the older, steadier men were allowed shotguns. In a wide arc they swept through the brush, yelling, stamping, poking, those in the lead confident in their high-top boots. They spent two hours covering the area; finally their noise died out in the distance as they moved on to the Harper spread.

Grace was subdued, but relatively calm; she had never expected much from life, and now she suddenly realized the advantages of having free use of her own time, own money, and own feelings—particularly the latter.

Morley felt better, too. The old, warm relationship between Grace and himself would rapidly be reestablished, he knew, and from now on he must keep Grace from getting involved with any more fortune hunters. Before Lang came along, a few of the locals had been coming around, but except for the sheriff, they were hardly eligible even to an undiscriminating woman like Grace. The sheriff, however, had never had a chance to push his advantage. Malcolm Lang, younger, far more smooth, and a lot more handsome, had moved in first. Sheriff Dawson was now safely married, the major reflected, with smug satisfaction. Just let any of those other clowns try it again! This time he'd know how much was at stake, and really put a spoke in their wheel, fighting hard—and dirty—if necessary.

The morning after the hunt, Morley was surprised, and slightly apprehensive, when Sheriff Dawson came upstairs to see him—a private matter, he told Grace, leaving her below.

"Good morning, Sheriff," the major said, apparently quite relaxed. "What brings you back here?"

"Well," the officer said, his pale gray eyes surveying the room, then pausing on the closet door, "we found something interesting on the snake hunt. It didn't mean anything to the others, but me, I was still chewing on just why a rattler would strike at a man drunk in a chair."

Morley felt his internal organs seethe under a massive injection of adrenalin and related hormones; but he kept his face impassive—or hoped so.

"Really," he drawled, "animals don't obey our rules, you know. Some guys sitting in classrooms decide what a snake can do, but nobody tells the snake. Isn't that so? You're an outdoorsman; you've seen the crazy things animals do."

"One thing they don't do," was the dry reply, "is wear belts. We found a fresh snakeskin, shed in the last day or two, and darned if it didn't have a nylon noose tight around the middle—part of a casting line: a twenty-pounder at that, big enough for a shark. You used to be quite a whiz at surf-casting and such, I heard tell."

The major's heart was pounding; this was bad—very bad. "What are you getting at?" he demanded, keeping his voice level.

"I was just thinking that if I looked in that closet, I might even find the line that noose came from; looks as if it broke."

Morley was raging, although his face was set. What an idiot he'd been! Goering so irritable, and even his color had been dull and dingy. Any fathead could have guessed the snake was ready to moult. The plan could have waited for another opportunity. But then how could he know the noose would break off? It was just bad luck, the kind no foresight could predict or control.

"Where does that leave me?" he asked, looking squarely at Dawson. "Am I under arrest? Just what are you going to do?"

"I know what I should do," the sheriff said, and the ambiguity of his reply shook Morley harder than the implied danger of a moment earlier.

"Your sister's a fine woman," Dawson said then. "It

would break her up all over, after losing Lang, to have
you tried for his murder. She'd lose you, too; we'd
have you cold, with that skin, and the line, and the
way Lang was killed. Yes," he repeated, "she's a
mighty fine woman; and this is a nice little ranch. You
probably haven't heard," he said, staring up at the ceiling in an abstracted way, "that my wife's getting a divorce. We never did hit it off very well."

The major was silent for a moment, although he
lusted to kill again. Then he said quietly, "She's a very
fine person, Grace. But I'm not sure she'll marry again;
she rather likes being free—after Malcolm."

"If you put in a good word for me, Dawson said,
"she'll come around. I'm no Lang; I'm easy to live with.
Good food and affection are what I need; then I'm the
nicest guy in the world. She thinks a lot of you. Anybody you plump for will have the inside track with
Grace." He fixed his gaze on the ceiling again. "Lots
of people go after snakes with a stick and noose. Nobody else on that hunt noticed that this was fish line.
For that matter, no law against using fish line to catch
a snake. There wouldn't ever have to be any questions.
A man doesn't stir up trouble against his own brother-
in-law; his wife wouldn't like that. 'Course," he added,
bringing his pale eyes down to Morley's, "I'd naturally
keep that skin in a safe place; it's a sort of curio. Good
for years, a dry snakeskin; and a man could always get
a new idea from it, something he missed at first, not in-
tentionally. It wouldn't have to work out like that, but
it could, and there's no statute of limitations on murder.
Like I said, if you talked to Grace—"

"I'll talk to her—in a few days," the major said heavily.

"Fine," Dawson beamed. "By the way, I like a drink,
too, just the same as Lang; but I never take enough to
pass out, and I don't aim to do any dozing near your
window. Still, maybe I'll keep all your fishing tackle
downstairs; it isn't as if you could use it yourself, and
I've always wanted some really good rods and reels.

Well, it's been nice chatting, but I'd better get down; Grace is making fresh apple pies."

Morley watched him leave in gloomy silence. After all his plans and hopes, he had managed only to exchange an albatross about his neck for a buzzard.

THE EYES OF A COP

by Edwin P. Hicks

Joe Chaviski couldn't sleep, so the big ex-detective hauled himself out of bed in Lodge No. 10, Happy Hollow Courts, at Pine Valley Lake, pulled on his clothes and headed for the restaurant. A dish of vanilla ice cream and a chat with Sam Willoughby might take his mind off those big bass he expected to catch in the morning, and then he could get some sleep. Funny how a man his age, with a thousand fishing trips behind him, still got stirred up the night before the thousandth and one foray after bass.

It was 10:15. A jalopy with an Oklahoma license plate was parked in front of the restaurant. The car was grimy with dirt and spotted with oil, and somehow didn't look "right" to him. Joe realized it was his old copper's instinct and grinned. It was hard to forget he was no longer a police officer, no longer a young man.

Joe plunked his 255-pound body on a leather-covered stool at the counter. The jukebox was making a racket, with some asinine drugstore cowboy singing through his nose a mournful ballad about a blonde siren who had taken him from home and loved ones.

Four crummy-looking individuals, two young men and two frowzy blondes in tight stretch pants and low-necked blouses, occupied the booth next to the jukebox.

Sam Willoughby wasn't there, and Mrs. Willoughby was red-eyed and extremely nervous when she placed Joe's order of ice cream before him.

"Oh, Joe," said Mrs. Willoughby, "I'm so glad to see you. Sam's gone home sick and I'm afraid it's appendicitis. I'm so worried about him."

"Why don't you close up this place and go to him?"

Mrs. Willoughby nodded toward the occupied booth. "Just as I was about to close up for the night, those four came in," she said. "I've just served them. I don't like their looks, and I'm afraid they'll hang on and on."

"Give me their ticket," said Joe. "If they need beer or coffee, I'll get it for them. You run on home to Sam. I'll close up."

"Would you, Joe?"

"Sure. And if you and Sam need anything—me to drive him to the hospital or anything like that—just let me know. I'm in Number Ten."

"Joe, you're a darling," said Mrs. Willoughby. She left at once.

Joe was absorbed in his ice cream and thinking about Sam Willoughby when one of the men shouted, "Hey, Fat! You in charge here?"

Joe turned and looked at the fellow. He was lean and bronze, his right ear had the mark of the fighter trade, flattened into a beautiful cauliflower, and his nose was out of line to the left. The other man was dark-skinned, with fiercely black hair.

"Yeah," Joe answered, keeping his temper. He didn't like to be called *Fat*. "I'm in charge. You need something?"

"Beer," said the bronzed one. "Beer all around and make it snappy."

Joe opened four bottles of beer and carried them over to the booth, two bottles in each of his big hands.

"That's a hell of a way to serve beer," said the one who had been popping off. "Don't you know any better than that, Fat?"

Joe grunted, added the amount of the beer on the check, and started to go back to the counter.

"You don't like to be called Fat, do you, Fat?"

"No, it doesn't go over so well with me."

"That's too bad." The tough slyly stuck out one foot to trip Joe as he turned. Joe stepped on the foot heavily, and the fellow yelled, then swore.

"Serves you right," one of the blondes said, laughing.

"Yeah? Well, we'll see who's laughing before we leave here."

They ordered more beer and kept the jukebox rattling with hill-billy music. Joe glanced at the clock. It was now 10:50. All the occupants of the cabins were sound asleep. There would be nobody else in tonight. He hoped they'd drink their beer and leave without any trouble.

They called for more beer. "This place closes at eleven," said Joe, as he placed the beer on the table.

"We'll leave here when we feel like it, Fat," said the young tough.

Joe added the price of the beer to the check and ambled back to his stool. Lucky he hadn't been able to sleep. No telling what would have happened if Mrs. Willoughby had been alone when this quartet showed up. Sam kept a .45 automatic in the drawer beneath the cash register, and no one was ever going to run over Sam, but Mrs. Willoughby would have been helpless. These four meant to cause trouble.

They were quarreling now over in the booth—the young hoodlum who had been rubbing Joe the wrong way, and one of the women who sat across the table with the dark one. The other woman was chiming in shrilly from time to time. They called the dark, silent man Pedro, while the other was Frenchy.

Now it was eleven o'clock, and Frenchy was hammering on the table and yelling for more beer.

"I can't serve you more beer. It's closing time," Joe said. "You people will have to leave."

"I said more beer!" Frenchy shouted.

Joe moved over to the table. "And I say pay up and get out!"

Frenchy came to his feet with surprising speed, considering the beer that was in him. The woman sitting beside him caught at his arm. He turned and slapped her.

Joe grabbed Frenchy by the collar, and the hood exploded a fist against his chin. The punch was a dandy, and Joe went back against the counter. He came back with startling speed and gathered Frenchy in his arms, squeezing him until the air sighed out of his lungs like a protesting accordion. Then Joe discovered he was fighting a wildcat. He had subdued one end, but the other was walking up him, kicking, scraping, stomping, kneeing! Joe threw Frenchy down and sat on his middle. He sank his great hands into both biceps of his opponent, until he could feel the bone beneath his fingers.

"Put the money for the bill on the table in the booth," Joe told the others, "and then get out of here. As soon as you get out the door I'm throwing this clown after you and closing up."

They placed the money on the table.

"Now get!" said Joe.

"Mister, you don't know what you're in for," said the woman who had been slapped. "You'll have to kill him. Why don't you go ahead. I'd like to see you kill him."

"Go on! Beat it!" said Joe.

They went out the door, the women clattering their heads off.

"They're right," said Frenchy. "You don't know what you're in for. I started wanting to tangle with you the minute I saw you come in this dump. Any man as big as you I want to take a poke at."

"Mister," said Joe, "I'm a retired police officer, and I haven't got any quarrel with you at all. Now I'm letting you up, and you leave here like a good fellow. I don't want to have to hurt you."

Joe got up and stood ready to spring at the tough if he still wanted to mix it. Frenchy turned and started for the door. The next thing Joe knew, a chair was hurtling toward his head, with Frenchy, heels first, right behind it. Joe sidestepped the chair but couldn't quite miss the heels. One foot grazed his stubby temple, the other struck his shoulder.

Joe twisted with the blow and got Frenchy from behind, wrapping one great arm around his belly and pressing down against the back of his neck with his forearm. He put on the pressure until he was afraid he would crush Frenchy's backbone. Then he hurled the body through the screen door and turned to slam the wooden door—and Frenchy was back, pummeling him in the face with slashing lefts. It was like backing a jackhammer with your chin.

The big man pawed the flashing left down with his own left and sent a sledgehammer right-cross into Frenchy's face. The blow only partly connected because the target was moving, but Frenchy went to the floor. Joe was after him, swallowing him up like an open umbrella, and he hit down at his opponent mercilessly. Some of the blows landed, but most of them were off target because two hard knees were banging against Joe's back, and the head rolling against the floor was like than of an old-time pug on the ropes dodging the knockout punch.

Joe Chaviski, veteran of the hand-to-hand combat that comes with thirty years on a police force, was a hard man to get riled. He had once killed a man who had gone berserk by breaking his neck with his bare hands—and had saved a carload of teenagers in so doing. Now no one's life was involved except his own, and he figured he could take care of that. So again he let Frenchy up from the floor.

It was a mistake! The battle started all over again— the giant heavyweight, who was getting along in years but who was surprisingly fast for his size, and the tough, scrapping middleweight who wouldn't quit!

Joe got his man down several more times, but he couldn't keep him there. Frenchy not only appeared to enjoy the combat, but also knew quite a bit about judo and was as fast as ever. The two women and the dark-skinned Pedro were back inside again, watching the fight and cheering first one, then the other.

Joe began to get tired. It was like fighting fifteen rounds at top speed and no stopping between rounds.

Now Frenchy was grinning! It seemed the more he was hit the stronger he got.

Joe was more angry now than he had ever been in his life. He yelled at the other man and the two women, "See if you can't make him stop! What the devil's the matter with him?"

"Kill him, big man! Kill him!" the woman who had quarrelled with Frenchy shouted, laughing.

Frenchy had the endurance of a lobo wolf. There seemed no stopping him. Joe's great fists sent him flying across the restaurant a dozen times, but Frenchy came rushing back.

Joe was panting now, his face cut, bruised, and bleeding. His left eye was almost closed. His chest, belly, and groin had been pounded and kicked. This fight couldn't go on much longer. It couldn't go on because he was going down—he, Joe Chaviski, who sometimes had handled a half dozen men at a time.

There was one more supreme effort in Joe. He caught the wriggling head of Frenchy in his left hand and smashed the grinning face with his right fist. This time Frenchy relaxed all over. He was out cold. He might even be dead! Joe didn't know. He was past knowing anything. Staggering drunkenly on his last legs, Joe dragged Frenchy to the door and hurled him out into the night.

Joe came blindly back through the door, and the two blondes ran to him and hugged him. "Our champion!" one of them said. "Frenchy's had that licking coming to him for months. I hope you killed him!"

Joe shook them off. He didn't have breath enough left to waste words. He tottered back of the counter, got the .45 from beneath the cash register, staggered out front with it in his hand.

"All right, get!" he said. "Get the hell out of here, all of you!" The gun was pointed at Pedro, who turned without a word and started for the door. Out of the corner of his eye, Joe saw the flash of the beer bottle wielded by one of the blondes, but it was too late to duck.

Someone was shaking him, and Joe was looking up at the clock, and the time was ten minutes before midnight! The man shaking him was a state patrolman, while an officer in plainclothes was by his side.

"Come on, Chaviski, wake up!" the state patrolman was saying. "What's been going on here, Joe?"

"I had one hell of a fight with a wildcat of a hoodlum, and one of his broads let me have it with a beer bottle."

"And how do you explain this?" asked the man in plainclothes. Joe recognized him as Sheriff Garton of Blakely City.

"This" was the body of Frenchy! There was an ugly bullet hole through the side of his head, another under his left arm.

The .45 automatic which Joe had brought from behind the counter was on the floor near where Joe's hand had been. The patrolman stuck a pencil through the trigger guard, lifted the weapon, and sniffed. It's been fired all right. Did you kill the man, Joe?"

"No," said Joe, "I sure didn't. I had finally put this guy they called Frenchy away after we'd been going it for about thirty minutes. I threw him out the door for keeps, then went around the counter and got Sam Willoughby's gun and was running out the other three, a dark-complected guy and two women, when this floozie comes up behind me and lets me have it with a bottle. They were all full of beer and had been quarreling. I figure it must have been this dark guy let Frenchy have it, then tried to make it look like I did it."

The back of Joe's head felt like it was about to come off. He placed his hand back there, touched a knot the size of a hen's egg, and drew the hand away, bloody. Joe steadied himself by holding onto a chair, looked about the place with glazed eyes.

Sheriff Garton got a first-aid kit out of his car and

bandaged Joe's head. A search of Frenchy revealed very little. There was a driver's license in his billfold made out to Henry Gazzola, Douglas, Arizona—probably stolen—and something like fifty dollars in bills. That was all. There were various tattoo marks on the arms, including the outline of a heart, with the initials "G.F." inside the heart.

The rest was routine. Joe accompanied Sheriff Garton to Blakely City, taking his own car, and a call was put in by radio for an ambulance to remove the body. The state patrolman remained at the restaurant.

Joe gave the Blakely City police a description of the two women and Pedro, and the license number of the Oklahoma car. True to his police training he had made a mental note of the license the moment he spotted the car in front of the restaurant. It was a Sequoyah County, Oklahoma, license. Radio messages to the sheriff's office there revealed that the license had been taken off a car in a parking lot four nights previously. In all likelihood they would steal another license plate before daylight, or even another car.

Nevertheless, routine roadblocks were set up at Texarkana, Fort Smith, Little Rock, Shreveport, Mena, and DeQueen, but the trio could leak through this broad net on a hundred back roads in the area.

In the meantime Joe told everything he knew to the officers at Blakely City, including the district head of the state police, Chief McCray of the Blakely City police department, the chief of detectives, Sheriff Garton, and deputy prosecuting attorney.

"Well, what do you think? Sounds like that bunch they want for that Springfield, Missouri, supermarket holdup, doesn't it?" Chief McCray said to the sheriff.

Garton nodded. They showed Joe an FBI report and prison pictures which had arrived just that day. Joe nodded. It was Pedro and Frenchy, all right. They were wanted for the $8,000 robbery of the Springfield supermarket some ten days before. The man called Frenchy really was one Gaspar François, alias Frenchy Beauchamp. He was a one-time pugilist, had traveled with the athletic show of a carnival, meeting and defeating all comers in boxing and wrestling matches, and had served one year in prison on a stickup conviction. He and Pedro were wanted for an Arizona bank robbery and for the Springfield job. Pedro Gonzales had an equally impressive record, and had served a three-year term on a manslaughter conviction.

Everybody was weary. The investigation would continue next day. Joe drove back to his cabin at Happy Hollow. His head hurt like the devil, and a couple of ribs felt like they were broken. His face was swollen and puffed. He ached in every bone of his body. Just the same, Joe felt a lot better after reading that report on Frenchy. Frenchy wasn't any ordinary punk at all— but a veteran pugilist and still in his physical prime. No wonder Joe was exhausted.

Joe moaned as he crawled into bed. He hurt all over, and his fishing trip had been all messed up by those hoodlums. In the distance, he heard a hoot owl sounding off—with the echoing answer of its mate. Frogs were booming in the button willow marsh that bordered a nearby cove. A fox was yapping on the hillside.

It was an hour before Joe got any sleep. He was thinking again that it was fortunate Mrs. Willoughby hadn't been left alone with that crummy quartet. No telling what might have happened. And he was thinking about the events of the night—thinking like a cop with thirty years of experience behind him.

Joe was up at seven o'clock. He showered, dressed, and looked out at the lake. The haze had already risen, and there was a slight ripple on the surface. It was just right for fishing, but there would be little fishing for him this day.

Both Mr. and Mrs. Willoughby were at the restaurant. "How about that appendicitis?" Joe asked.

Sam Willoughby grinned sheepishly. "Guess it was a case of the old-fashioned bellyache," he said. The floor had been scrubbed clean. Willoughby nodded toward it.

"Thanks, Joe. Thanks for taking care of Sue—and for everything."

One or two fishing parties were breakfasting, chatting away happily over ham and eggs about what they expected to catch when they put out on the lake. Joe glanced at them curiously. Real fishermen would have been out on the lake before sunup. Apparently they weren't aware of what had happened in the restaurant during the night. None of them had heard the two shots which had killed Frenchy. They had been fast asleep.

Willoughby brought over a couple of cups of steaming coffee and sat facing Joe in the booth. "Barest kind of a mention of the shooting, Joe, on the early-morning news from Blakely City. Too early for their local newsman, I guess."

Mrs. Willoughby came over for Joe's order. "Good morning, Mr. Chaviski," she said, "and thanks!" The heavy coating of face powder she had used didn't conceal her red and swollen eyes.

"Just want to tell you, Joe," said Willoughby, after she had taken the order, "that I'm sorry about what happened last night. They might have killed you. I'll always be grateful that you took care of Sue."

Joe didn't say a word. He just looked at Sam.

"What's the matter, Joe?"

Joe continued looking squarely at Sam without replying.

"Damn it, Joe! What's the matter with you?"

"I thought you were my friend," said Joe.

"I am your friend."

"Then why did you try to frame me last night?"

"What do you mean, try to frame you?"

"Why did you plant that gun in my hand?"

"Who says I planted that gun in your hand?"

"I do," said Joe.

Willoughby dropped his gaze.

"When Sue told you what was about to happen down here, you returned to the restaurant and parked at the back. You came in after they had knocked me out—"

Willoughby now looked Joe squarely in the eye. "You've got me dead to right, Joe," he said. "I come in through the back, just as they cleaned out the cash register—those two women and the guy. They run out the front door when they saw me. I went for the gun where I kept it, but it wasn't there. Then I saw it on the floor by you and picked it up. About that time this other guy I hadn't seen before comes through the door like a madman. He picks up that broken bottle they had bashed over your head and was down over you quick as a cat. I yelled at him, but he was going to cut your throat, so I let him have it twice and he just curled up. Then I put in a call for the sheriff, telling him that I was one of the fellows staying in a cottage who had heard the shooting. I stayed and watched over you until I figured the sheriff was about due, then I drove back home with my lights off all the way."

"That still doesn't answer my question," Joe said sternly. "Why did you try to frame me?"

"I figured you wouldn't have no trouble getting out of it, Joe, you being a respected officer and all that. I guess I made a mistake."

"You sure did," said Joe. "Except for that one little technicality of putting my prints on the gun I don't think you'd have had any trouble at all. A coroner's jury would have cleared you. Now you're in a jam."

"Joe, will you help?"

Joe reached over and pressed Sam's hand. "Sure, Sam. After all, you saved my life."

"Sue will be mighty glad to hear that, Joe. She's been all cut up about it. But how did you know it was me and not that dark guy or one of those gals?"

"I didn't know it until I was going to sleep after I'd been over to Blakely City this morning. Something came to me—something I'd been worrying about all the time. You had set up all the chairs we'd knocked over in the scrap, put the place pretty much back in order. I noticed something odd the moment the state patrolman and the sheriff got me up on my feet off the floor, but I had been hit on the head, and I guess

I wasn't thinking right at the time. What gang of hoodlums ever cleaned up a place after a fight?"

"Well, I'll be darned, Joe. I guess I just did that through habit while I was waiting. I didn't even know it until you told me just now!"

CHEERS

by Richard Deming

I stayed out until 11:00 P.M., hoping the landlady would be in bed by then, but she had waited up, and her door opened just after I had sneaked past it.

"Mr. Willard!"

I flinched, then turned around to face her. She stood in her doorway, fat arms folded across her ample bosom, her eyes blazing.

"Yes, Mrs. Emory?" I said meekly.

"It is the seventeenth!"

"Yes, ma'am, I know we promised the back rent today, but the fight we had scheduled was postponed—"

"Fight, schmight," Mrs. Emory interrupted. "I don't think you're ever going to have another fight. You and Mr. Jones either pay up or get out. Tonight!"

"At this hour? Be reasonable, Mrs. Emory. I guarantee that by noon at the latest—"

I was interrupted again, this time by the front door opening with a bang. I recognized my roommate and manager by his lanky legs. That's all you could see of him because the upper part of his body, and even his head, was hidden by the huge pile of packages he was carrying.

I moved forward to relieve him of part of the load. In one of the paper bags I took from him, bottles clinked in an interesting manner.

Ambrose Jones peered around the remainder of the packages. "Ah, Mrs. Emory," he said with amiable formality, "you're looking particularly revolting tonight."

If the packages hadn't already given it away, his greeting would have told me that Ambrose had fallen into money. He always insulted the landlady when he was flush. His formal tone also told me he was half-stoned.

Mrs. Emory knew the symptoms, too, and ignored the insult because she knew it meant our back rent was forthcoming. She used her pass key to open the door, and we both dumped our packages on the nearest twin bed. With a flourish Ambrose drew out a roll of bills.

"Here you are, my benevolent gargoyle," he said, counting out four twenties into the landlady's outstretched palm. "Two weeks back rent and two weeks rent in advance."

Mrs. Emory sniffed and left the room. Ambrose locked the door behind her and fanned the roll to show me that the twenties had been its lowest denomination. Most of the bills were fifties.

"How soon can we expect cops to be beating on the door?" I asked.

"Now, Sam," he said reproachfully, "this represents the advance on a business transaction. One thousand dollars, less what I spent for purchases and paid to Mrs. Emory. We have four thousand more coming at the conclusion of the deal."

The only thing I could think of was that he must have matched me with the champ and guaranteed that I would take a dive. No, that couldn't be it. Why would the champ need a guarantee? I hadn't lasted a full round in two years and hadn't even had a fight in six months.

While I was going through these mental convolutions, Ambrose was opening packages. There were clothes for both of us. There were cold cuts, cheese, rye bread, pickles, caviar and smoked oysters. There was champagne, Scotch, bourbon and various mixes.

Ambrose stacked the comestibles on the dresser.

While he sorted out the clothing, his and mine, I made myself a thick sandwich.

Then I asked, "Who do we have to kill?"

"A fellow named Everett Dobbs," he said brightly, and poured champagne into two water glasses.

I said, "Kidding aside, Ambrose, what's the deal?"

He raised his eyebrows at me, and popped a couple of smoked oysters into his mouth which he swallowed before saying, "I told you. Our client is a Mrs. Cornelia Dobbs, a handsome but fading nymph of middle age who has tired of her husband. I met her in a bar. After buying me several drinks she broached the subject of murder. She seemed to be under the impression I was a criminal type because the place was Monty's."

That was understandable. Monty's is a waterfront bar where a large percentage of the clientele *are* criminal types.

"So you conned her out of a grand," I said.

"Conned her? I accepted an ethically binding advance. Are you accusing me of being dishonest?"

I found shot glasses in the top bureau drawer, opened a bottle of bourbon and poured. We had several more each, along with cold cuts, cheese, caviar, smoked oysters and pickles. As we reveled, Ambrose explained the arrangements he had made in more detail.

Everett Dobbs was a retired real-estate speculator with about half the money in the county. He and his would-be widow lived in one of the huge homes in the Glen Ridge area. Dobbs spent most of his time at the Glen Ridge Country Club, however, and that's where Cornelia Dobbs wanted us to "take" him.

According to Cornelia, her husband left the club promptly at eleven every night, almost invariably alone, and drove home. She had furnished Ambrose with a description of the man's car and its license number. We were to wait in the parking lot, waylay him, and drive him off in his own car. One of us would drive Dobbs' car, the other would follow in the jalopy Ambrose and I jointly owned. We would arrange some kind of fatal accident. Cornelia, of course, would have arranged an unbreakable alibi.

I didn't doubt he was completely serious at this particular moment, and I was quite sure there actually was a Mrs. Cornelia Dobbs and that Ambrose had agreed to kill her husband for five thousand dollars, but Ambrose tended to lose his sense of perspective when he was drinking. I figured that when he groped through the red haze of next morning's hangover, he would be appalled at himself.

In fact, I thought I might have a problem convincing him to keep the thousand-dollar advance. Cornelia could hardly demand it back without risking considerable trouble for herself, but my manager had a peculiar code of ethics. He was capable of arranging a fixed fight, but he always stood by his word.

I was still turning over in my mind arguments in favor of keeping the advance and telling Cornelia to get lost when Ambrose passed out.

Ambrose awoke with the hangover I had predicted. When he could open his eyes all the way without bleeding to death, he gave me a weak smile and elbowed up.

"Smoked oysters don't mix very well with champagne, I guess."

"No," I agreed. "I'm sure it was the oysters."

He got up, wrapped a robe around his lanky frame and went up the hall to shower and shave. When he came back, I made the same trip.

Ambrose has remarkable powers of recuperation. He was dressed and clear-eyed by the time I got back. We had no conversation until I finished dressing.

Then I said, "You won't have to return the money. She couldn't possibly do anything about it."

"Return it? Why should I return it?"

"I mean she can't go to the police."

He frowned at me. "Why should she go to the police?"

"For fraud. When we don't kill her husband."

He examined me as though searching for the hole in my head.

I said patiently, "You're certainly not serious about becoming a professional killer."

"For five thousand dollars? Of course, I am. I explained it all last night."

"You were drunk last night. We're not killers."

"We're not anything," he said. "You're not a fighter. You're an ex-fighter, which makes me not anything either. I'm an ex-fight manager."

There must have been a lost look on my face, because he said in a more kindly tone, "This is our chance, Sam. With a stake we could find another fighter. I'll manage and you can train him."

"But murder, Ambrose!"

"Aw, come off it, Sam. You killed a man in the ring once."

"An accident," I said. "It's not the same. They put you in the gas chamber for murder."

"Only if they catch you. Do you know why most murderers get caught?"

"Sure. Because they're not as smart as cops."

"Most aren't," Ambrose agreed. "Statistically, eighty percent of the murders in this country are committed by friends or relatives of the victims. The cops have it easy with these cases. They simply check back on all the victim's associates, and eventually they have to come to the one who pulled the trigger or swung the axe or dropped the poison in the coffee."

"So eventually they'll get to us."

Ambrose gave his head a slow shake. "How? We've never even seen him and he's never seen us. There's no point of contact for the cops to check back on."

That made sense, but it takes a while to adjust to the idea of murder. I said, "They always suspect the wife. Suppose she breaks down and fingers us?"

"She won't break down. She'll have a perfect alibi, and besides, it's going to look like an accident."

I fingered one of my cauliflower ears while I thought this over. Finally I said, "Suppose he doesn't come out of the club alone?"

"Then we wait until the next night and Cornelia rigs another alibi."

I had only one last question. "How do we collect the other four thousand?"

"She's to bring it to Monty's tomorrow night."

"I'm still not convinced," I said. "Let's go get some breakfast, and maybe you can convince me while we're eating."

He did.

We spent the day in plans and preparations. We drove out to Glen Ridge Country Club and looked over the parking lot. Then we drove over the route Everett Dobbs would take home and found a beautiful spot for an accident.

The road wound over Glen Ridge, a small mountain with a hairpin turn right at the crest, protected only by a wooden guard rail. Below the guard rail the mountainside sloped down at a sixty-degree angle to another section of the winding road nearly fifty feet below.

"They'll think he cracked up on the way home," Ambrose said. "Cornelia says he drinks a lot, so it'll just look like another drunk who missed a curve."

We got out to the country club at nine that night, just in case Everett Dobbs left early. Ambrose parked the jalopy and we got out to look for Dobbs' car. Cornelia had described it to Ambrose and had given him its license number, so we had no difficulty finding it even though it was quite dark by then and there were some fifty other cars on the lot.

As soon as we located it, Ambrose drove the jalopy into a vacant slot right behind it, and we settled back to wait.

Ambrose had brought along a fifth of Scotch for himself and a quart of bourbon for me in order to relieve the tedium. We also needed it to quiet our nerves.

"Maybe we'd better slow down on the hootch," I suggested.

Ambrose frowned at me in the darkness and took

another swig of Scotch. "I'm as sober as a sphinx," he said.

At 10:00 P.M. a lone figure came from the direction of the clubhouse and weaved in our direction. He was a tall, lean man in a dark suit, and his gait indicated he was cock-eyed out of his skull.

"If that's Dobbs, he's an hour early," Ambrose said.

"From the looks of him, the barkeep probably cut him off. He wouldn't have lasted until eleven."

The man put a key into the door lock of the car we were watching.

"Guess this is it," I said. "I can handle this joker alone. You just follow."

I got out of the car and was surprised when I staggered slightly. Straightening, I went over to where the tall man was still fumbling with the lock.

"Having trouble?" I asked.

"The keyhole keeps moving, old man," he said. "Would you mind seeing if you can hit it?"

He handed me the keys. The keyhole *was* moving, I noticed, but I managed to slip the key into it on the second try.

"Bravo!" the tall man said when I pulled the door open. "May I buy you a drink for your trouble?"

I decided getting him to go along willingly would be simpler than slugging him. "Sure," I said, "but not here. I know a better place."

"Fine," he said with enthusiasm. "Any place good enough for my friends is good enough for me." He thrust out his hand. "My name is Dobbs, old buddy."

I shook the hand. "Willard," I said. "Sam Willard, pal o' mine."

"Delighted, old man. And now the keys, please."

"Maybe I'd better drive," I said. "I know where this place is, and you don't."

"Be my guest," he said, offering a little bow and losing his balance.

Preventing him from falling on his face by catching him, I helped him into the car, then slid behind the wheel.

The engine purred beautifully. As I pulled off the lot, the jalopy chugged along behind us. Dobbs promptly went to sleep. We reached the hairpin turn at the top of Glen Ridge without incident. It was just beyond the crest, so that there was a slight downgrade to it. I parked on the very crest and Ambrose parked behind me. There wasn't another car in sight.

Dobbs was still sleeping, and I was afraid he would wake up if I pulled him over under the wheel. I figured nobody would be able to tell he hadn't been behind the wheel anyway, after a drop of fifty feet.

Ambrose came up, weaving slightly, as I climbed from the car. Leaving the door open, I shifted into drive, released the emergency brake and reached in to press the accelerator with my hand. I pressed it gently, just enough to start the car rolling. Then I shifted into neutral, pulled out my head and slammed the door.

It was about forty feet to the guard rail. The car picked up speed nicely and crashed through the wooden barrier as though it were cardboard. The sound of vegetation being torn out by the roots ended in a tremendous crash from below.

We raced back to the jalopy, Ambrose backed and turned, and we headed back the way we had come.

"Maybe we should have kept going the other way," he said worriedly as we reached the next turn. "We have to drive right past where it landed, and maybe it's blocked the road."

"It probably just bounced and kept going," I said. "There's another small drop on the other side."

We rounded another curve, and now were right below the hairpin turn. A fender, a wheel and a lot of broken glass littered the road. Presumably the rest of the car had continued on across the road, over the next bank and down into the underbrush below us. We couldn't see down there because it was too dark.

Ambrose slowed to five miles an hour in order to edge past the debris. A tall figure slid on the seat of his pants from the undergrowth sloping upward to our right. Ambrose braked to a dead halt.

The man picked himself up, brushed off his pants and staggered over to the window on my side of the car. His clothing was pretty well torn up, but otherwise he seemed unharmed.

Leaning his head into the car, he said, "I say, gentlemen, I seem to have had a bit of an accident. Must have gone to sleep."

He was looking straight at me with no sign of recognition. Apparently he was one of those drunks who blank out, because he obviously had no recollection of our previous encounter.

"I'm not exactly sure where I am," he said in a tone of apology. "Do you happen to know?"

"Glen Ridge," I said.

"Oh, yes." He glanced around vaguely. "I recognize it now. I say, do you suppose that's part of my car?" He was looking at the smashed green fender.

"Uh-huh," I said. "No point in looking for the rest. I doubt that it will run." I got out of the car. "Get in."

"Why that's very nice of you gentlemen," he said, climbing into the middle. "May I buy you gentlemen a drink?"

"We have one," I said, handing him the bourbon bottle.

He took a grateful swig as Ambrose started the car. When he handed the bottle back, I took a swig, too. Ambrose lifted his Scotch bottle from the floor and had a drink.

"What now?" I asked Ambrose.

"I'm thinking," he said.

"I think I must have been heading for the country club," Dobbs said, "but I can't go in these clothes. Would you gentlemen mind dropping me at my boat?"

"What boat?" Ambrose asked.

"I keep it at the Lakeshore Yacht Club." Suddenly his face brightened with inspiration. "Do you gentlemen enjoy night fishing?"

Even as dark as it was I could see the interest in Ambrose's face. "What kind of boat do you have?"

"Just a small one. A twenty-five-footer."

Ambrose and I exchanged glances, both thinking the same thing.

"You mean you'd like to go fishing tonight?" Ambrose asked.

"If you gentlemen have the time to be my guests."

"We'll take the time," Ambrose said.

The pier of the Lakeshore Yacht Club was well lighted, and we could see about fifty boats, ranging from skiffs with outboard motors to cabin cruisers, docked in individual slips. None of the other owners seemed to share Dobbs' enthusiasm for night fishing, because there wasn't a single car in the parking area facing the pier.

Our host directed us to park in front of slip number twelve. The boat was a graceful little cabin cruiser with an enclosed bridge. A registration number and the name *Bountiful* was painted on the bow.

Ambrose carried the Scotch bottle as we clambered aboard. Dobbs and I had finished the bourbon en route. By now he was so snockered, we had to help him aboard.

Dobbs showed us below by opening the hatch and falling down the ladder. I was the next down, but I held onto an iron handrail and made it erect. I lit my lighter, spotted a wall switch and flicked on an overhead light. By the time Ambrose had joined us, I had helped Dobbs to his feet.

"Thanks, old man," he said. "I'll have to get those steps fixed."

There were four bunks and a couple of cupboards in the cabin. Dobbs opened one of the cupboards and took out a couple of fishing rods. "Bait's topside," he said, dropping the rods and staggering to hands and knees.

I helped him to his feet again as Ambrose collected the rods. Ambrose carried them tops while I assisted Dobbs up the ladder. Dobbs collapsed in a canvas chair on the stern deck and immediately went to sleep.

"You know how to run this thing?" Ambrose asked.

"I've handled boats," I said. "Not on fresh water, but it shouldn't be any different than salt water. I'll take a look."

I climbed up to the wheelhouse and, with the aid of my lighter, found the control-panel lights. It took my eyes a time to focus, but eventually I figured out the purpose of the various controls. I started the engine, let it idle and switched on the running lights.

Ambrose climbed up into the wheelhouse. "You familiar with the harbor?" he asked.

"I told you I'd never been out on the lake before."

"No, you didn't. You just said you'd never handled a boat on fresh water."

"All right," I said. "No, I'm not familiar with the harbor, but the channel will be marked with buoys."

Ambrose peered aft. "That looks like a seawall out there. Don't run into it."

I looked that way and dimly saw a long concrete breakwater across the mouth of the harbor. A pair of blinking red lights about fifty feet apart bobbed in the water at the near end of it.

"I know how to navigate," I growled. "Go cast off."

He started down the ladder frontward, then changed his mind and backed down, holding onto the iron handrail with his free hand.

After some fumbling with the line he finally cast off. A moment later I backed from the slip, swung the boat around and headed at low speed for the lighted buoys marking the harbor entrance.

"Go out a couple of miles," Ambrose said.

My navigation must have been a little rusty, because I scraped one of the lighted bouys as we went by. I missed the other by a good fifty feet, however.

Then we were beyond the seawall, in open water. There was only a slight roll, but it brought a groan from Ambrose. I opened the throttle and headed straight out from shore.

Ambrose had said to go out a couple of miles, but I couldn't seem to focus my eyes on the compass, and I was afraid if I got too far out to see the harbor lights, I might get turned around. About a half mile out I shifted into neutral, let the boat drift and went down on deck. I figured nobody as drunk as Dobbs would be able to swim a half mile.

Dobbs was still asleep. Ambrose was hanging onto the stern rail and breathing deeply. His face was pale.

"Feel better?" I asked.

"I'm all right. How far out are we?"

"Far enough," I said, and lifted Dobbs from his chair. He nestled his head against my shoulder like a baby.

I heaved him over the stern. There was a splash, a sound of floundering, then a sputtering noise.

"Man overboard!" came a strangled shout from the darkness.

The shout came from several yards away, because the boat was drifting rapidly. I went tops, engaged the clutch and swung back toward the harbor. Ambrose came up to stand beside me.

As we neared the blinking red lights of the buoys, I thought of something. I said, "Aren't the cops going to wonder how Dobbs got so far out if we leave his boat docked.

Ambrose patted my shoulder. "Luckily you have a manager to do your thinking for you, my sinewed but brainless friend. After we land, we'll aim the boat back out to open water. Eventually it'll run out of gas and be found drifting. When Dobbs' body is washed up and the autopsy shows he was full of alcohol, it'll be obvious he fell overboard in a drunken stupor."

I wasn't so brainless that I couldn't see a big hole in this plan. We were almost to the marked channel now. I cut the throttle way down, swung in a circle and began to back toward the end of the seawall.

"What are you doing?" Ambrose asked.

"You can't aim a pilotless boat like you do a gun," I said. "There isn't a chance in a thousand I could hit the channel if I started it out from shore. It'd crash right into the *inner* side of the seawall and give the cops something to wonder about. So we'll land on the seawall, aim it outward from here, then walk along the wall to shore."

I was making sternway at too sharp an angle. I shifted to ahead, pulled forward several yards and tried again. I had to maneuver several times before I got it just right, but I finally managed to slide the boat gently against the end of the cement wall with its bow pointed outward.

About a dozen seagulls roosting on the wall flapped away when the hull scraped the cement.

Ambrose jumped onto the wall and held the boat there by the rail. I could hear the cement grinding a little paint off, but it wasn't doing any serious damage.

I set the rudder so the boat would go straight out from shore, spiked the wheel, engaged the clutch, and gave it just enough gas for headway. Then I scrambled down the ladder. Ambrose had been unable to hold the boat against the thrust of the propeller, and there was already a three-foot gap of water between me and the wall when I mounted the rail.

I made a mighty leap, landed on the wall and crashed into Ambrose, knocked him down. Another flock of seagulls a little farther on flapped into the air.

Ambrose climbed to his feet, examined his hands, then tried to peer around at the seat of his pants. He took out a handkerchief and wiped his hands.

"This wall's just been painted," he said.

"That's not paint," I told him. "It's seagull manure."

A revolted expression formed on his face. He wiped at the seat of his pants with the handkerchief, then tossed it into the water. I led the way along the seawall to where the harbor shore curved around to meet its far end. Roosting seagulls rose at our approach and settled again on other parts of the wall. As we neared the wall's end, I spotted a pair of blinking red lights and came to an abrupt halt.

"What's the matter?" Ambrose asked.

"I hope not what I think. We'll know in a minute."

We went on and discovered that what I had hoped against was true. The blinking red lights I had seen were on buoys marking another channel. There was seventy-five feet of water between us and shore.

Ambrose said bitterly, "I should never let you think."

"So we'll get wet. We'll just have to swim for it."

"I can't swim," Ambrose announced.

After some unfriendly discussion, we finally solved that problem. Ambrose held onto my belt while I breast-stroked across the seventy-five-foot channel. We climbed out on what seemed to be the public dock. A few fishing tugs were tied up to it, but nobody was around.

"At least I got my pants clean," Ambrose said, craning around in an attempt to see his seat.

It was about three-quarters of a mile along the curving shore back to where our jalopy was parked. We sloshed along without conversation. Although it was a fairly warm night, we were chilly in our wet clothes. Occasionally I could hear Ambrose's teeth chattering.

As we reached the Yacht Club pier, I spotted the running lights of a boat just entering the harbor by means of the channel we had used. The lights moved in our direction.

We both halted in front of slip twelve and watched the *Bountiful* slide smoothly into its slot. The running lights went out and a tall, lean figure descended to the deck and tied up. Then he saw us standing there.

"Hello, fellows," Dobbs said cordially, examining our wet clothes with interest. "You get a ducking too?"

"Uh-huh," Ambrose said morosely.

"Lose your boat?"

He had blanked out again. He didn't even remember us.

I said, "Yeah."

"Too bad," Dobbs said with sympathy. "I was luckier." He indicated his own sopping clothing. "I'm not sure just what happened, because I was drinking a little. First I knew, I was in the water and separated from the boat. You can bet that sobered me up. I swam around for a devil of a long time before it swung back right by me at a speed slow enough for me to climb aboard."

"You're a lucky guy," Ambrose said sourly, his mouth drooping.

In an apologetic tone Dobbs said, "I'd offer you a change of clothes, but I only have one on board. You live far from here?"

"Clear downtown," Ambrose said.

"Well, if you wait until I change, I have a place near here where you can dry out. It's not my home, but it has a dryer in it, and something to drink."

We decided to wait.

Dobbs disappeared below. Ten minutes later he reappeared wearing sneakers, white ducks and a turtle-neck sweater. When he stepped onto the pier he staggered slightly, but instantly righted himself. I realized that while his cold bath had sobered him considerably, he was still about half-stoned.

He glanced around the parking area and looked puzzled when he saw no car but ours.

"How the devil did I get here?" he asked. "I just remembered my car's in the repair shop."

He must have a vague recollection of the accident, I thought. Neither of us told him his car wasn't in a garage, but was spread over a considerable area at Glen Ridge.

"Must have taken a taxi," he decided. He thrust out his hand to me. "My name's Dobbs."

"Willard," I said.

When he offered his hand to Ambrose, Ambrose said, "Jones."

"Delighted," Dobbs said. "How'd you lose your boat?"

"Capsized," Ambrose said briefly. "It was only a skiff and we were inside the seawall."

We let Dobbs sit in the back of the jalopy so that we wouldn't get him wet. He directed Ambrose to drive three blocks south to Main Street, then two blocks west.

"Pull in that driveway," he said, pointing.

The entrance to the drive was between stone pillars. On one of the pillars was a sign: *Dobbs Funeral Home.*

Dobbs had Ambrose park by a side entrance and we all got out.

As our host fiddled with a key, I whispered to Ambrose, "I thought this guy was in real estate."

"Retired," Ambrose whispered back. "Guess he's gone into another business."

Dobbs got the door open and led us into a small foyer. An open door off the left side revealed a business office. Dobbs opened a door to the right, flicked on a light switch and led us down a flight of stairs to the basement.

We passed through a room full of empty caskets into another room where there was a sink, a couple of metal tables on wheels and a counter along one wall containing implements of various kinds. I guessed this was the embalming room.

From a cupboard Dobbs took two folded white cloths which looked like small sheets, except that the material was heavier. He handed one to me and one to Ambrose.

"Sorry I haven't robes to loan you while your clothing dries," he said, "but you can wrap yourselves in these."

We emptied our pockets on one of the embalming tables, stripped off our clothes and wrapped the sheet-like cloths around us like togas. Dobbs carried our clothing, including our shoes, into what seemed to be a service hall off the embalming room. A moment later we heard a laundry dryer start to rotate.

When Dobbs came back, Ambrose asked, "What are these things we're wearing?"

"Shrouds," Dobbs said.

I didn't exactly shudder, but I hoped he had set the dryer on high.

Dobbs went over to a cabinet, took out three water glasses and a bottle of Scotch. I noted that there were several other bottles in the cabinet. He set the glasses on one of the embalming tables, poured a stiff jolt into each glass and held onto the bottle.

"Let's go in here where it's more comfortable," he

said, and led us into a comfortable little den. Dobbs
set the bottle on a desk and took an easy chair, Ambrose took another and I sat on the sofa.

"Cheers," Dobbs said, raising his glass.

We raised ours in salute. Dobbs tossed off his whole
drink. Ambrose and I each took only about half of
ours.

It went that way for the next half-hour. For every
ounce of Scotch Ambrose and I drank, Dobbs put away
two. At the end of the half-hour the bottle was empty.
Dobbs tried to get out of his chair and found that he
couldn't.

"I say, old man," he said to Ambrose, "would you
mind getting us a fresh bottle?"

The swim had considerably sobered me, but I was
beginning to feel a little fuzzy again. Ambrose seemed
perfectly sober, though, when he rose, clutched his
toga around him and went into the embalming room. I
noticed he carried the empty Scotch bottle with him.

"How long does that dryer take?" I asked Dobbs.

"Dryer?"

"You put our clothes in the dryer, remember?" I
said. "How long does it take?"

"Oh, your clothes. Yes, of course. They're out in
the dryer, old man."

"How long does it take?" I asked patiently.

"The dryer? About forty-five minutes. Wasn't there
another gentleman with us a moment ago?"

"He went after more Scotch," I informed him.

"He did? That was unnecessary. There's plenty in the
embalming room." He attempted to focus his eyes on
a wristwatch, gave up and asked, "What time is it, old
friend?"

My watch said eleven-thirty, which surprised me.
Then I realized it was stopped. It wasn't waterproof.

"I don't know," I said. "I'd guess about twelve-
thirty."

Ambrose came back carrying two bottles. He handed
one to Dobbs, poured drinks for me and himself from
the other. Dobbs poured his tumbler nearly full. We

all drank, Dobbs, as usual, pouring it all down in one gulp. He looked surprised.

"Was that Scotch?" he asked in a squeaky voice.

He picked up his private bottle and looked at the label. His eyes wouldn't focus on it, so I went over and looked at it.

"Scotch," I verified.

Dobbs gave a relieved nod and poured himself another glassful. I went back to the sofa, sat down and looked at Ambrose. He was looking at Dobbs.

Ambrose raised his glass and said, "Cheers."

Dobbs drained his glass and looked surprised again. "Odd," he said, staring at the glass.

Ambrose got up, wrapped his toga about him and went over to pour the man a third drink. Dobbs merely continued to stare down at it thoughtfully.

We sat there in silence for about ten minutes. Ambrose and I finished our drinks and Ambrose poured two more. Dobbs hadn't sampled his third one.

"Cheers," Ambrose said, raising his glass.

Dobbs raised his very slowly. It took him a couple of minutes to let it trickle down his throat, but he managed to put it all away. His arm came down with equal slowness, resting the glass on the arm of his chair.

Ambrose asked, "How long does that dryer take?"

Our host didn't answer. I said, "Forty-five minutes."

"Then our clothes should be done," Ambrose said.

The dryer had stopped. Our clothes were bone dry, but our suits were wrinkled and the shoes were stiff.

When we had dressed, Ambrose carefully refolded the shrouds and replaced them in the cupboard. We picked our pocket items from the embalming table and stowed them away.

"What about him?" I asked, jerking my thumb toward the den.

"He should be done, too."

A trifle unsteadily he walked into the den. I trailed along. Dobbs sat in his chair with a fixed smile on his face. Ambrose went over and shook him. There was no response.

Ambrose tried to lift the glass from his hand, but couldn't. He tried to pry the man's fingers loose, but they were gripping the glass too tightly.

"What's the matter with him?" I asked.

"He drank about a fifth of embalming fluid."

I gave the man in the chair a startled look. "You mean he's finally dead?"

"Cold as a carp. We'd better get him out of here."

"Why?" I asked.

Ambrose thought this over, weaving slightly. Presently he said, "I think we'd better collect on this tonight and then blow town, instead of waiting until tomorrow night. And what better proof of accomplishment can we show than this corpse?"

It was my turn to think matters over. Somehow his suggestion didn't strike me as very wise. If we left Dobbs where he was, it seemed to me the cops would assume he got too stoned to know the difference between Scotch and embalming fluid, which was more or less what had actually happened. Driving around with a corpse in the car seemed asking for trouble, but as Ambrose had pointed out, what better proof could there be than the corpse?

Ambrose said, "Take that glass out of his hand."

I tried, but I couldn't bend his fingers.

"The hell with it," Ambrose said. "Just carry him out to the car."

He was stiff as a frozen steak. When I heaved him into my arms, he remained in his seated position, his right arm thrust out in front of him and the glass still clutched in his hand.

Ambrose picked up the Scotch bottle we had partly emptied, plus the one containing the embalming fluid. He switched off the den light and carried the two bottles into the embalming room.

He set down the Scotch bottle and dumped the embalming fluid in the other one down the sink. I stood with the rigid body of Dobbs in my arms as he rinsed out the bottle and dropped it into a waste can. Then he picked up the Scotch bottle and preceded me into

the casket room, switching off the embalming room
light as he went through the door.

At the top of the stairs he flicked the light switch to
turn off the light in the casket room. When I had carried
Dobbs into the foyer, he closed the door behind me.
The foyer light had been on when we entered, so we
left it that way. Ambrose set the spring lock on the
side door before pulling it closed behind us.

I set Dobbs in the rear of the jalopy, where he sat
erect, smiling frozenly and thrusting his glass out before
him. I climbed in front and Ambrose backed out of the
driveway.

It was a long drive to the home of Everett and Cornelia Dobbs. When we passed the place where the car
had crashed, someone had pulled the wheel and fender
off onto the shoulder, but the road was still littered
with glass.

It must have been 2:00 A.M. when we finally arrived.
A curving drive led past a swimming pool which had
underwater lights. Since no one was in the pool, I assumed the lights were left on all night as a safety pre-
caution so no one would fall into it in the dark.

The house was a two-story brick. Ambrose parked
right in front of the porch and we both went up to the
door. Through a window we could see a night light on in
the front room. Ambrose rang the bell.

"Suppose she's not alone?" I said.

"She will be. She outlined her plans to me in detail.
She was having some women in for bridge to establish
her alibi. She estimated they would leave about midnight, and she was going to ask the woman who had
driven the others here to call her when she got home
so she'd know everybody got home safely. That would
cover her until about twelve-thirty, then she planned
to go to bed until the police awakened her to report
the accident."

Several minutes passed and Ambrose had rung the
bell again before it finally opened. A bleached blonde
of about thirty-five in a housecoat peered out.

"Ah, Mrs. Dobbs," Ambrose said with a formal

bow which nearly threw him off balance before he managed to right himself. "This is my partner, Sam Willard."

She barely glanced at me. "What in heaven's name are you doing here?"

"Reporting mission accomplished. We have the evidence in the car."

She came out on the porch and looked from me to Ambrose. "That's impossible."

"Look in the back of our car," Ambrose said, making a grand gesture in that direction.

"What are you talking about?" she asked crossly. "Everett phoned me from the club. He loaned his car to Herman and stayed there all night."

She went down the steps and peered into the back seat. Her eyes grew saucer size.

"Herman!" she said. "What's the matter with him?"

We had followed her down the steps. Ambrose said, "Herman?"

She swung on him. "That's Everett's younger brother, you fool! The man I intend to marry. What have you done to him?"

One thing about Ambrose: even snockered to the eyebrows he could always think on his feet. He said soothingly, "He's merely drunk, madam. We'll see that he gets home safely. Sorry we erred. He was getting into your husband's car and he said his name was Dobbs, so naturally we assumed he was your husband."

"Why did you bring him here anyway?" she snapped.

Ambrose was still thinking on his feet. He said, "We meant to undress him, put on his swim trunks and drown him in the pool."

"Shut up!" she hissed. "Herman doesn't know anything about my plans! Or at least he didn't."

"He can't hear you," Ambrose assured her. "He's passed out."

He gave her another formal bow, rounded the car and slid under the wheel. I scrambled in next to him. Ambrose backed the car, turned and drove back down the driveway. Gazing back, I saw Cornelia Dobbs still glaring after us.

Ambrose pulled over to the curb as soon as we hit the street, cut the engine and lights.

"What now, genius?" I asked.

"We wait until her lights go out again."

All but the night light went out a few minutes later.

"Okay," Ambrose said. "Lift him out."

I got out, reached in back and lifted the stiff body into my arms. Ambrose led the way up the driveway and over to the swimming pool. There were a couple of canvas lawn chairs next to it. Ambrose had me set Herman Dobbs in one.

He had brought along the Scotch bottle. He stood contemplating Herman Dobbs' frozen smile for a moment, then poured the outstretched glass half-full.

"Cheers," he said gloomily. "Now let's get the hell out of here, pack our stuff and head south."

CRIME DOESN'T PAY—ENOUGH

by Ed Lacy

Bill Jackson was a little guy who lived by his sharp wits. True, he worked as a shipping clerk, but that was merely an avocation to insure his eating regularly while he spent all his time entering contests. Bill won a number of things—1,000 cakes of soap (which he finally sold to a grocer for twenty dollars) shirts, a weekend in the country, candy, books, a TV set, several watches, and many odds and ends. Bill was a very hard worker, and devoted a great deal of time to each contest. One day he won a $50,000 puzzle and ceased being a shipping clerk.

Unfortunately, a prize like that came to the attention of the income-tax people. Bill was shocked to find himself giving Uncle Sam $28,000, plus another four grand to the state tax office. $18,000 remained of his prize. And since he was now living in a fast style he was completely unaccustomed to, this was melting fast, much to his dismay.

Being an intelligent young fellow, Bill told himself, "Contesting is better than working, but as a pure business venture—it's lousy. Something wrong with a business where you only keep less than 40 percent of the take. So I'm through with contests. I have to find me something calling for a sharp mind, and which will let me hold on to 100 percent of what I make."

Since Bill was spending his money rapidly, he was constantly cashing checks at the bank. Several times he noticed the manager of a large supermarket making deposits of $15,000, and more, on Monday mornings. The manager was one of these physically big men who are often stupid-brave; he never had a police guard. For the first time in his life, Bill turned his wits to crime. The profits from a holdup would be all his, and being a smart type, he decided not to go in for guns or violence. Quietly, for several weeks, he cased the Monday morning delivery to the bank of the market's weekend receipts.

The manager opened the store at 8:30 A.M. and customers were allowed in at 9:00 A.M. For the next hour, the manager was busy in his office. Promptly at 10:00 A.M. he placed the money in a small suitcase and drove to the bank. Bill decided the money would have to be taken just before the manager stepped into his car.

Next, Bill turned his imagination to ways of outsmarting the police, to his getaway. For days, he scouted the area around the supermarket. Several blocks east of the store was an entrance to the river parkway. Part of this was still under construction and for a short stretch a temporary wooden fence separated the road from the river. Bill studied the fence and the river. The roadway was only five feet above the surface of the water— which had to be deep, for large tugs often traveled the river.

Exactly as in a contest, Bill carefully wrote down all the possible factors, gave each much thought before coming up with a working solution.

A national holiday was going to fall on the following Sunday, meaning the banks would remain closed Monday, although the market would be open. By Tuesday the manager should have a heavy deposit ready. Once he had the day set, Bill investigated makeup, spent $20 experimenting with powders and dyes, disguising his hair and face. Then Bill purchased an Aqua-Lung for $150, and $10 worth of cork. On the Friday before the three-day weekend, he bought some cheap secondhand clothing for $30, stole some license plates and let himself be sold a secondhand car for $500, which looked terrible but was in good running order. Bill bought the car under a phony name.

Early Tuesday, he disguised his face with realistic-looking warts and scars, added a moustache, and using a water dye, turned his hair a mild red. Then he drove his regular car to an isolated spot across the river, left it there—locked—with towels, shopping bags, and a change of clothing in the back seat. He was back on the city side of the river by 7:30 A.M., where he picked up his beat-up car, made certain the Aqua-Lung and the cork were hidden in the back, then parked it directly in front of the supermarket. Bill was sweating a little, some cop might notice the number of the stolen plates, pull the rug out from under the whole idea. After shoving a small length of pipe in his pocket, Bill took a walk.

At 8:20 A.M., the store manager arrived, angry to find this old car in his usual parking space. He was forced to park down the street, out of view of the supermarket windows and employees—as Bill had planned.

At 10:00 A.M. the manager left the store, the suitcase heavy with money. As he neared his car, a cheaply dressed redheaded young man, walking with a limp, came up behind him. Seemingly asking him an address, the man shoved a paper in front of the manager on which was written "THIS IS HOLD-UP!" and at the same time shoved the end of the pipe against his coat pocket and into the manager's fat side. The redhead said with a heavy accent, "I got .45, blow your kidney out. One wrong move, me shoot. You be smart, man, hand me bag and keep walking. Five minutes you walk, no look back, or I blow your head off. Money insure, you wish die for insurance company, you great fool!"

The manager was big, but not a big dummy. He gave the redhead the bag and kept walking up the street. Quickly, but casually, Bill carried the bag to his old car, drove off. When he passed the manager, he heard him yelling for the police. Bill slowed up a block away, carefully cranked the window down, securely tied the corks around the heavy bag. Waiting until he heard the police sirens behind him, for he had *to be certain the cops saw him,* he headed for the river highway.

Turning into the parkway, Bill paused again to fasten the Aqua-Lung on his back. Then, with the radio patrol car gaining on him, Bill raced up the empty parkway. Nearing the wooden fence, he seemed to lose control of the car—which shot over the curb, crashed the fence, struck the water with a great splash, and sank.

The water impact hadn't dazed Bill as much as he had expected. Before the car reached the muddy river bottom, Bill had his mask on and was breathing air from the tanks on his back. Towing the money bag, he calmly swam out of the car window and crossed the river under water. Letting the fast current carry him along, he surfaced now and then to check his position. Finally, he saw his car, made for shore—still under water. Removing the Aqua-Lung, Bill tore off one of the rubber tubes and threw the Lung back into the river, knowing it would sink. Scrambling up the bank, he yanked off the car key tied to his belt, and dripping wet, got in the car and drove off.

Minutes later, he turned into an empty lot—as if having tire trouble—quickly changed in the back seat to dry clothes, wiped off the remains of his make-up, then leisurely returned to his own apartment. He carried two shopping bags, full of wet clothes, and the suitcase.

Emptying the money in his bathtub, Bill ripped the clothing bag to pieces. When these were dry, he put them into bundles of greasy garbage he'd been saving for this purpose and dropped everything down the hall incinerator.

After locking his door, Bill had the delightful experience of counting his damp loot—$21,158 in cash, plus $3,531.72 in checks and money orders, which he tore up without a second's hesitation and flushed down the toilet. Bill had his radio on and heard about the supermarket robbery . . . that the thief had been drowned when his speeding car plunged into the river. The police were dredging for the car, but due to the depth and strong currents, they thought there was little chance of ever finding the money or the body. Bill gave out a satisfied yawn—now here was a sound business! With an investment of some $710 he had taken in over twenty-one grand, with little chance of being caught, and absolutely no tax bite.

The evening papers carried a more detailed story. The police said the car had come apart on being pulled out of the river, but the patrol-car driver stated it had been an old Chevy with a busted left tail light and an uncompleted paint job. The manager was busy studying mug shots of redheaded criminals, etc. etc. Bill casually put the money in a steel trunk, left it in his closet, and went out to do the town—as usual.

He did the same thing for the rest of the week, but on Saturday night he had the feeling he was being followed. He was. The old man who ran the used-car lot and who had sold Bill the Chevy, told him, "Let's you and me have a beer, young fellow. I'm bushed, running all over town looking for you. When I read about a Chevy that somebody had started to paint and never finished and that had a busted taillight, I knew it was the heap I'd sold you. And when I remembered how you hadn't argued about the price, I figured maybe you wasn't at the bottom of the river. I'm not greedy. Papers say you scored $25,000. Well, $10,000 will ruin my memory."

Bill said he'd be at the parking lot in the morning, with the money. He spent the rest of the night thinking. Be no point in running; if the guy gave the police his real description, he'd be collared sooner or later. Being on the run had never been part of his plans. He also knew blackmail is rarely a one-shot, that he'd have to keep paying the rest of his life.

Sunday he kept the appointment, handed over $10,000 as the happy car-lot man hysterically swore he'd never trouble Bill again. Bill drove across the river to a shabby little town he'd heard of, but had never visited, stopped at a dreary bar. Over a few beers, he mentioned to the barkeep the trouble he was having with the brother of his brother-in-law and how he wanted somebody to work him over for $100. He did this act in several crummy bars before he was introduced to a hard-looking character who said he'd beat anyone senseless for $300, cripple him for $800—cash on the barrelhead. Softly, Bill asked what the killing rate might be.

The tough guy talked around it, but added, "For nine big bills, I'd knock off my own brother!"

Bill said he'd think it over, return the following night. In his room he weighed all the angles—as he did false clues in a contest. Would the killer blackmail him? No, because if Bill refused to pay, the killer couldn't squeal to the cops because that would mean the chair for him. Even if the killer was caught, what could he tell the police? He didn't know Bill's name, or even the town where Bill lived. And as far as the police knew, Bill had no motive for wanting the car-lot owner killed. It was risky, but not too risky. Nine thousand was expensive, but he had to get the car-lot owner off his back.

The next night Bill took a bus across the river, met the killer-for-hire, made a deal. He said he could only raise $8000, so that the killer wouldn't think he had a rich cat on the string. Bill would finger the victim—right away—and tear the eight grand in half. The killer would get one half that night; Bill would bring him the second half of the torn money when he read of the old man's death.

The hard character said he liked a clean-cut business deal. And what were they waiting for?

They rode the bus back to the city, then another bus to within a few blocks of the car lot. They walked the rest of the way—only to find the lot a mass of charred wreckage. A passerby explained the owner had gone on a long binge, blew up the oil stove in his office, killing himself.

Full of relief, Bill walked the killer into a deserted

alley, said, "The deal is off. I'm giving you $500 for all the trouble you've gone to and—"

Yanking out an ugly gun the hood said, "Naw! You got the dough on you! Hand over all the eight grand!"

"Why, you dirty crook!" Bill said, keeping his hands up as the thug took the money from his pocket. Bill was too small to be a fighter, but suddenly he went crazy with blind anger. He swung on the man, who was now busy counting the folding money.

It was a lucky punch, dropping the killer; his gun fell from his hand, but not the eight thousand. He immediately rolled over, scrambled to his feet, and took off still clutching the money. Grabbing the gun, Bill started after him. The man turned a corner, dashed across a street heavy with traffic and into the path of a truck, which squashed him as if he'd been a bug.

Standing on the sidewalk, Bill saw the blood of the dead man mix with the money. He was horrified. Finally, he pocketed the gun and walked away.

Bill is back to trying to win contests, for out of $21,000 he'd only kept under $300, which is worse than any tax bite. So he's given up crime for good and is working very hard on a big puzzle deal . . . in jail.

A cop, you see, quite accidentally saw Bill throwing the gun down a sewer, and so now Bill is doing a year and a day for carrying a concealed weapon. But being able to devote almost 24 hours a day to the puzzle, he feels certain to win big, real big.